BISON
BOOKS

The Trickster

AND

the Troll

VIRGINIA DRIVING HAWK SNEVE

University of Nebraska Press

Lincoln and London

⊗

First Bison Books printing: 1999

Library of Congress Cataloging-in-Publication Data.

Sneve, Virginia Driving Hawk.

The trickster and the troll / Virginia Driving Hawk Sneve

p. cm.

Summary: Iktomi, a Lakota trickster, and a troll from Norway meet and become competitors,
helpers, and friends as they try to hold on to the native ways that are being abandoned as more
people settle across America.

ISBN 0-8032-4261-1 (cloth: alk. paper).

ISBN 0-8032-9263-5 (paper: alk. paper).

1. Iktomi (Legendary character) – Juvenile fiction. [1. Iktomi (Legendary character) – Fiction.

2. Trolls – Fiction.   3. Norwegian Americans – Fiction   4. Dakota Indians – Fiction.

5. Indians of North America – Great Plains – Fiction.]   I. Title.

PZ7.S679TR 1997   [FIC] – dc21   96-36879 CIP AC

For Joan, Bonita, Madeline, and Nickolas

CONTENTS

Contents

AUTHOR'S NOTE

My family is bicultural. Vance, my husband, is of Norwegian descent; I am Lakota, more commonly known as Sioux. Our children, when young, called themselves "Sioux-wegian."

The duality of their heritage inspired this story, and its characters are from the folk tales of both cultures.

Iktomi is the trickster figure of the Sioux, one of many such figures found in just about all Native American tribes. Iktomi is called "Spider Man" by the Sioux, and though he no longer resembles the spider, he continues to weave webs of trickery and deceit.

Tricksters lie and cheat, and are often selfish gluttons. They exaggerate and boast of how they get the best of lesser creatures—including humans. They never accept responsibility for their actions but always get their comeuppance. Yet tricksters never learn from their misadventures. Iktomi of this story is no exception.

Trickster stories are told to entertain. Indeed, Iktomi's antics are amusing even though he usually gets in trouble because of his actions. The tales are teaching tools that show children what happens when one misbehaves.

Traditional storytellers begin a trickster story, "Iktomi was going along. He was hungry . . ." and I begin this story in a like manner.

Within this story, I have woven together bits and pieces of many trickster tales. Iktomi has special powers. He can understand and speak to other creatures—so he can communicate with a troll.

Trolls come from Scandinavian folk tales. Norwegian immigrants brought their tales, customs, and values with them to homesteads in the upper Midwest. Descendents of Norwegian settlers recall grandparents telling of a troll in the rain barrel or a troll in the haystack. Trolls could be mischievous, wicked, and cruel or gentle, kind, and helpful. These traits are also common to Native American trickster figures.

Another commonality to both cultures was the pressure brought upon them by mainstream U.S. society to become Americans. The response of the two groups was a traumatic change in lifestyle.

The American Indians were forced into change. They unwillingly gave up many elements of their heritage. Their children were taken from their homes and sent to boarding schools where they were forbidden to speak their native language. They stayed away from home until their education was completed. They lost much of their cultural identity and often were accused of being "white" when they went home.

Author's Note

The Norwegian settlers voluntarily chose to become American, to anglicize the spelling of their names, and to speak English rather than Norwegian. Those who kept to the ways of the old country were ridiculed by Americans who made up the dominant society.

With the loss of language many cultural elements were also lost or submerged beneath an "Americanized" facade. This story tells of this loss through the eyes of folk heroes. They were exiles who were submerged in cultural denial until a new generation became nostalgic for a way they never knew.

Today there is an awareness that we live in a multicultural nation and that we can learn from each other to enhance our own world.

My thanks go to my personal readers: my mother, Rose Posey, my son, Paul Sneve, and my neighbor and friend, Duane Ellingson, past president of the Sons of Norway Borgund Lodge #52 in Rapid City, South Dakota. Their suggestions helped me give life to the trickster and the troll. Also, I thank Dr. Carl Sunde, Foreign Language Department, South Dakota State University, who helped me with the Norwegian words and phrases used in this book. Most of all, I thank my husband, Vance, whose encouragement kept me writing and whose Norwegian stories inspired this one.

The Trickster and the Troll

ONE

Iktomi

Iktomi was going along. He was hungry, but he carried no bow, quiver, or spear to hunt for game. Neither did he have a sharp pointed stick to dig wild turnips or onions. No, Iktomi would not hunt or dig for his own food — not if he could help it. He would go hungry until he found animals or fowl he could fool into being his meal. But best of all, Iktomi liked pitting his wit against the Lakota. He enjoyed tricking humans into giving him food.

Mi Lakota, ne Lakota. "I'm Lakota, you're Lakota," declared a meadowlark.

"Where are the Lakota?" Iktomi called, but the lark chirped its statement and flew away from the trickster. The bird knew of Iktomi's wily games — games that often ended with Iktomi eating his playmates.

Hungrily, Iktomi's eyes followed the lark, while his empty stomach rumbled in loud complaint. Iktomi snatched berries from shrubs along his path, but he would not stop to gather enough to still his complaining stomach. He wanted meat, or fish, or duck.

"Mmm," sighed Iktomi, "duck roasting over a fire. Mmm," he licked his lips as his mind pictured the fire with grease spattering. So vivid was the image that his nostrils quivered and twitched. *Sniff, sniff* went the nose in all directions, but it smelled nothing.

"Oh! Stupid nose!" Iktomi cried, and he gave his nose a hard slap.

"Ow!" Iktomi yelled, but he swatted his nose again. "How dare you smell roasting duck where there is none! Ow!"

Iktomi howled, but he continued to scold his nose. Iktomi never accepted the responsibility for any unpleasantness, even if he was the cause. He always blamed others—even parts of his own body.

So Iktomi jumped and howled and ran and cried until his foot caught in a clump of grass and he fell.

"Oooh," he sobbed. "Now the earth catches my foot and throws me down." His hand pounded the grass and a sharp stem jabbed his thumb. He glared at the spot of blood welling from the wound. "Poor thumb," comforted Iktomi and stuck it in his mouth.

Exhausted and weak from hunger, Iktomi lay still, sucking his throbbing thumb. Suddenly his wiry frame tensed; he pressed his ear to the ground, ignoring the sharp grass sticking into his cheek.

The earth vibrated beneath his body. Iktomi felt and heard it hum louder and louder until he quivered with the thudding tremors. A large creature was approaching.

Iktomi's eyes narrowed as he thought, "Is it *tatanka?*" and his mind raced with plans to start a prairie fire to trap the buffalo or run it off a cliff.

"No," Iktomi whispered as the thuds shook the earth. "It is a two-legged." His eyes widened in alarm. "*Mahto?*" he wondered. "No, the bear is seldom in the prairie. But what other two-legged walks with such ponderous steps?" He closed his eyes and listened; suddenly the thudding stopped.

Iktomi did not move his head, but his eyes flew open and roamed wildly in their sockets looking for whatever beast had caused the ground to tremble. The eye near the ground saw only grass and busy ants. The other saw a large twitching shape almost touching Iktomi's nose, which wrinkled and tried to pull away.

Iktomi stared at the object. "What is it?" His eye studied the odd form and recognized a cracked and broken nail over a dirt-encrusted big toe. Still, Iktomi would not lift his head. His eye rolled as far back as it could and saw stiff black bristles on the top of the toe.

"It's a human!" Iktomi's mind exclaimed in terror. "A giant human!"

A strangled squeal squeaked past the thumb in Iktomi's mouth. The huge toe jerked away. Iktomi slowly turned his head, rolled onto his back, and looked up.

TWO

Troll

Nei da! wailed Troll. *Jeg går meg will!* "Oh, no! I am lost!" Desperately Troll gazed at the tall grass that surrounded him in all directions.

"Nothing to see," Troll moaned and squinted his eyes at the cloudless, bright sky. "Just sky, grass, and sun."

His eyes ached from the endless glare. His nose, cheeks, and brow smarted from sunburn, as did his hands and arms dangling from tattered sleeves.

Shaggy hair protected his neck and ears, and a tangled beard covered his chin. He rubbed his itching neck and moaned as salty perspiration stung the prickly heat rash that tormented him.

Troll wiped his hands on his sweat-stained shirt and lifted it to cool his damp skin. Burrs and grass seeds had clung to his shapeless trousers and worked through the cloth to pierce his legs.

His feet hurt, his toes were bruised and sore. From head to toe, Troll was dirty, hot, and miserable.

He licked his dry lips and yearned for water. Heat waves wavered above the tall grass; sunspots glittered and danced above a tantalizing mirage of a cool stream.

Troll blinked to dispel the vision and saw only grass flowing to the horizon. Which way should he go?

Wearily he headed toward what seemed to be a higher mound on the flat plain. From that vantage maybe he could sight trees and, hopefully, water. Troll lowered his head and painfully lumbered through the grass, occasionally glancing though slitted lids to mark his way.

Du vet sa lite du, sang the meadowlark to the plodding giant. "You know so little, you!" Troll heard the birds sing. "Yah," he agreed and stopped to watch the bird fly away. "I know very little about this country."

THREE

A Giant Encounter

Wearily, Troll lowered his big head. He blinked his eyes, "What?" He wasn't sure if he was really seeing a person below him on the ground. "A man?"

Whatever it was had a thumb in its mouth, and its nose almost touched Troll's big toe. Troll wiggled the toe and then jerked back as the creature gave a startled squeal and rolled away.

On the ground, on his back, Iktomi stared up into the eyes of the tallest being he had ever seen. Iktomi and Troll pondered each other with mouths open and hearts pounding.

A wet bead of sweat slid down Troll's nose and splattered Iktomi's forehead. The drop dribbled into the trickster's eye, and it blinked at the salty sting. Iktomi wiped his face, then sprang to his feet. "How dare you—you monster—spit on Iktomi!" His fear forgotten, Iktomi confronted the troll. "How dare you disturb Iktomi's rest?" He shook his fist at the giant's stomach.

Troll stood, amazed and perplexed. He gazed at the small man who shouted and waved his arms.

Bits of grass dangled in Iktomi's braids. His headband hung askew, its lone feather flopped over his ear. "Naked?" Troll wondered and then saw the flaps of leather about the smaller being's loins. "Ahh," he sighed, recognizing what he saw.

"*Indianer,*" Troll whispered. This was one of those red men whom his humans feared. Slowly Troll relaxed. There was nothing frightful about this small person who yelled bombastically while he jabbed at Troll's belly.

Troll listened to the language not at all like Norwegian, and at first did not know what was being said. He concentrated until he understood.

"Who are you? What are you?" Iktomi demanded, poking a fist into the giant's middle. When Troll did not answer, Iktomi punched harder.

"You are ugly, Giant! You are dirty! You stink!" Iktomi paused to get his breath, then let out a startled squawk as two huge hands squeezed about his middle. "Awk!" cried Iktomi as he was swung up until he was face to face with the troll.

"Aarrh!" roared Troll. "And you are a skinny bit of—of—," he stammered. Unable to end his comparison, he roared again. "Aarrh!"

Iktomi closed his eyes against the hot blast in his face as the giant's bellow thundered over the plains. Iktomi gasped, struggled, and pushed down on the restraining hands.

7

"St—aawk!" Iktomi protested, and the roar subsided. Iktomi slowly opened his eyes and gaped at the red, sweaty face and bloodshot blue eyes so near to his. "Blue?" he thought and relaxed. "Ahh, this is only an oversized *wasicu*."

Iktomi had met white men in his travels and found that they were easy to trick. Now, his mind began scheming ways to use this encounter to Iktomi's benefit.

"O Great One," the trickster's voice assumed a soothing, hypnotic tone that usually managed to placate and persuade any creature. "Forgive me. I did not recognize you as one of the great ones. Persons of your greatness do not often honor the plains." Iktomi smiled and patted the hands about his waist.

Troll cocked his head at the person in his hands, and his grip loosened.

"Oh," sighed Iktomi, "thank you, Great One." He took a deep breath. "I should have known that a great one such as yourself would be merciful and kind. BUT!" he shouted as the giant's mouth opened. "Please, do not roar again!" Then he soothed, "Not that your voice isn't pleasing to hear, but *tatanka* will be disturbed."

"Tah-ton-kah?" questioned Troll.

"Yes," Iktomi went on to explain, "the other great ones of the plains. The buffalo is my humans' center of life."

"Center of life?" Troll wondered what the small one meant.

"Yes, hmm," Iktomi cleared his dry throat. "O Great One, why don't you put me down? I'm sure you are as hot as I am. Put me down and I will take you to a *ble* nearby where we can refresh ourselves."

"Bl—," Troll started to ask, then understood the new word. "Lake? Water?"

"Yes," Iktomi answered, delighted that he had recognized the giant's need. "Water. Cool, sweet water."

Slowly and gently, Troll lowered his hands and set Iktomi on the ground.

"Thank you." Iktomi rubbed the smarting skin where the giant had pinched his waist.

"Water?" Troll repeated. "Are there trees by the water?"

"Oh, yes," Iktomi pointed and led the way, "just a short walk, over there. Tall trees that will shade us from the sun. Come."

Troll lumbered after the lithe figure, wiping sweat from his brow and licking his dry lips.

Iktomi trotted and dodged to avoid the giant's heavy steps. "Clumsy beast!" he thought. "Now I know why all of the game and the Lakota have disappeared. This ugly one has frightened them away."

The two made their way through the grass that reached Iktomi's shoulders. But Troll looked over the trickster's head and saw trees, then sparkling water. He surged ahead of Iktomi and in two strides reached the lake.

Iktomi paused on the knoll above the lake to see a flock of

ducks soar out of the water as Troll plunged into its coolness. Iktomi's stomach growled in complaint. Troll's dive made waves that drenched Iktomi and knocked him onto the sand.

"*Witko!*" Iktomi was furious. "Fool!" he yelled, struggling to his feet. He helplessly watched the ducks fly away.

But Troll, wallowing in the shallows, gulped and drank until Iktomi feared the giant's thirst would empty the lake. "Ahh," Troll sighed. Delighting in the cool wetness, he waded and splashed until the bottom dropped away and he sank.

"Ho, *witko!*" Iktomi was gleeful. "You should drown, you clumsy—" But Troll sputtered to the surface and waded ashore. He wrung water from his beard, thoroughly drenching Iktomi.

Iktomi, awed at the sight of the massively dripping giant, did not object to being soaked. "See, Great One," he said, his voice gently persuasive. "Isn't this a pleasant place to which I have brought you?"

Troll nodded, peeled off his wet shirt, wrung it, and hung it on a tree branch.

Iktomi scampered away from the wet giant to the base of a stout tree. He cleared stones and twigs from the sand. "Sit," he invited. "Rest."

"Hmm," Troll wearily lowered himself to the sand and leaned against the tree, which creaked upon its roots but supported the giant. Troll closed his eyes.

FOUR

Ducks and Introductions

"Look at the ugly *wasicu,*" Iktomi's mind scoffed. "His little toe won't fit into my moccasin." Iktomi measured his foot against the sleeping giant's. "Ugly!" Iktomi shuddered at the hairy, firmly muscled legs stretched out on the sand. He moved closer to the bearded face, studying the sunburned nose and cheeks not covered with hair.

Wisps of mustache stirred under cavernous nostrils. Troll snored, snorted, gasped, coughed, and rolled over. Iktomi jumped out of the way as Troll tucked one hand beneath his bearded chin and rested the other on his chest.

"*Hinh.*" Iktomi was amazed and awed at the heavy arms. "Despite his ugliness, this giant has strength," Iktomi's mind mused. "He is so strong, he doesn't need a weapon—perhaps we can persuade him to hunt?"

"Later," Iktomi's hot, weary body signaled. "Think about it later." He turned away from the sleeping giant and waded into the lake.

Iktomi drank and bathed. He floated on his back. Delighting in the coolness, he relaxed.

"Ahh," Iktomi gazed at the clouds drifting across the blue above. As he rested lower into the lake, water seeped over his head and into his nostrils. He coughed and slapped at the water. "How dare you try to drown me?" he scolded, but he choked on water that filled his open mouth.

He waded to shore, complaining and wringing his hair. As he walked along the shore, the warm breeze felt cool as it dried his body. He sat near the sleeping Troll and his eyes closed.

Iktomi and Troll slept; the lake settled into glassy stillness and the ducks returned.

The quacking flock circled and touched down. Iktomi's alert ears heard and his eyes opened. When he saw the ducks his stomach growled with hunger. "We must catch all of the ducks," Iktomi's mind schemed.

"Feet, legs," Iktomi willed, "be quick and quiet!" His body tensed to rise. "Wait!" his mind commanded, and he watched the ducks swim single file to the shore and waddle into a circle on the sand. Turning their heads from side to side, they preened, spread their wings, and rhythmically bobbed their tails in a waddling circle.

"They're dancing," Iktomi's mind said, it formed a plan.

Slowly, quietly, Iktomi rose. Carefully he lifted Troll's shirt from the tree and stepped backward up the hill, his eyes never leaving the ducks. He watched them as he spread the shirt on the ground, pulled up grass, and piled it on the shirt. He tied the shirt into a bundle, threw it over his back, and walked down to the lake.

"*Hau,* brothers," Iktomi greeted the ducks. At the sound of his voice, they stumbled and fell over each other. "Don't be alarmed," soothed Iktomi before they took flight. "Don't let me disturb your dance. I only need a drink of water before I go on my way." He grunted, staggered, and struggled as if it were difficult to lower his bundle to the shore.

Iktomi's hypnotic tone calmed the ducks. They watched as he knelt to drink, one hand tightly grasping the pack.

"Why does Iktomi have such a large bundle?"

Curious, their fear gone, the ducks moved closer to the mysterious bundle. "What's in your pack?" they asked.

Iktomi ignored the ducks and continued to drink. The ducks crowded near, some even daring to peck at the bundle. Iktomi jerked his head up and threw his arms protectively around the bundle.

"Don't touch!" he warned. The ducks quacked in alarm.

"Shh," calmed Iktomi, and he cautiously peered into the knotted shirt. "Good," he nodded, "they're all here." Iktomi's bewitching smile beamed over the flock.

"What?" cried the ducks. "What is all there?"

Iktomi's mouth opened in feigned surprise at the ducks' curiosity. "Why, this is my bundle of songs," he said, peering into the shirt.

13

"Songs?" the ducks waddled nearer.

"Magic songs." Iktomi's voice was quiet, but it hummed with hypnotic power. "I sing them only for my friends who wish to have a ceremonial dance. These songs are full of mystery."

"We are your friends, Iktomi. We want to dance, but we have no songs of our own. Please sing for us."

"Hmm," Iktomi pondered. "I don't know. Are you really my friends?"

"Oh, yes, yes," chorused the ducks.

"Hmm," Iktomi looked into the eyes of each duck. Their quacks stilled under his gaze. "My friends always do what I tell them."

"We will!"

"Very well," Iktomi decided. "But you must do everything I tell you. These are magic songs and a bad thing will happen to you if you don't obey!"

The ducks quacked their agreement. Iktomi stood and selected a place to dance on the shore. "Form a tight circle," he instructed, and the ducks waddled into each other, hurrying to obey. Iktomi stood in the center making sure all of the flock was in place. "Now, I'm going to take a song from my bundle. Be quiet and close your eyes. You must not open them or the magic will be lost before I can sing the song."

The ducks squeezed their eyes shut. Iktomi bent over the shirt, rustling the grass as he untied it. "Mmm, which song?" he muttered loud enough for the ducks to hear. "Oh, here's a good one," he exclaimed, cupping his hands tightly to keep the song from getting away. He stood, tall and fierce, and studied each duck to make sure no one was peeking.

"Now, I will sing while you dance," said Iktomi, his voice deeply dramatic. "But remember, you must keep your eyes shut until the end of the song. If you open your eyes while I am singing," his voice threatened, "your eyes will turn red!"

The ducks trembled under Iktomi's spell but nodded their heads.

"Aay, aah," Iktomi sang. Willingly, the ducks stepped about the circle, their wings spread and their heads and tails bobbing in tempo to Iktomi's hypnotic rhythm. Their eyes tightly shut, they did not see Iktomi dump the grass and spread the shirt on the sand as he sang. The enchanting song enticed them to dance, and not one of the plump ducks protested as Iktomi grasped each slim neck. No surprised squawk came as necks were wrung and dead ducks dumped onto the shirt. Iktomi worked quickly, not missing a beat as he sang, and the ducks danced and died.

"A—A—AW," a bass voice rumbled in discord to Iktomi's song. The trickster's tune faltered and he looked about to find the source of the noise. "The giant!" Intent on getting a meal, Iktomi had forgotten the sleeping troll who was now yawning and stretching awake.

The spell wavered, ducks bumped into one another. Frantically, Iktomi sang louder and faster, but the ducks opened their eyes.

"Awk!" they squawked in horror at the sight of their dead

brothers. "Fly!" they quacked, flapping until their wings lifted them out of Iktomi's reach.

"Look! Look!" the horrified ducks cried to one another as they soared over the lake. "Our eyes are red!"

Below, an angry Iktomi shook his fists. "I told you so!" he yelled, pleased that his magic had worked.

"What are you doing with my shirt?" Iktomi jerked about at Troll's questions and found the giant glaring and pointing at the shirt piled with dead ducks.

Iktomi saw that there were enough ducks for a satisfying meal, which he would have to share with Troll. "Why, my friend," Iktomi soothed, "I was using your shirt to keep sand out of our evening meal."

"Let us build a fire and we'll have roast duck—a feast!"

Troll was hungry. If necessary, trolls could go without eating for long periods, but they still needed food. So the giant gathered dry wood while Iktomi dressed the ducks. He said nothing but was impressed with the ease with which Iktomi struck sparks from two rocks, igniting a small heap of dry grass. Soon ducks were spitted on green twigs around a hot fire.

After the meal, Iktomi and Troll lay on the sand. Troll belched and patted his stomach. He had almost forgotten what it was like to have a filling meal.

"Well, Great One," Iktomi said, sensing the giant's contented mood. "It's good that you are feeling better."

Troll nodded and belched.

"Let us become better acquainted," Iktomi's voice was friendly. "I am Iktomi, the wise one of the Lakota," he said, ignoring the voice in his head that chuckled at Iktomi's description of himself.

"All the Lakota respect me for the good I do them," Iktomi went on, paying no attention to the laughing voice of his conscience. "Now tell me, Great One, what manner of human are you and from where have you come?"

"I am not human," Troll answered in a quiet rumble. "I am a mountain troll."

Iktomi was astonished. "Not human?" he asked. "And what is a troll? And how can you be from the mountains? I have been to the mountains but have never seen you before."

"I am a troll," the giant repeated, "but not from the mountains in this country. My mountains are so high that they make those in this land look like anthills."

"What?" Iktomi exclaimed. "Anthills? My Paha Sapa, the black mountains of the Lakota, have towering peaks!" But he was too curious about the troll to argue. "Where are your mountains?" he asked.

"In Norway," Troll sadly answered. "I once lived for many hundreds of years on my own mountain in Norway." A tear slid down his cheek.

"What?" Iktomi cried again. "Hundreds of years? Is that what you said?" At Troll's nod Iktomi jumped to his feet. "I too have lived for so many winters—years as you say—that I do not know the number." Then solemnly Iktomi offered his hand to Troll.

Troll took the small hand and stared at the slim figure before him. His memory stirred. Long ago in Norway he had enjoyed listening to his humans tell stories, not only of trolls but of other ageless beings who lived in other lands. "Are you an elf?" he asked.

"Ell-luf?" Iktomi did not understand.

"A gnome? A fairy?" Troll asked, but Iktomi shook his head.

"NO!" Iktomi lost his patience. "I am Iktomi! The Lakota trickster!" This time the laughter of the voice in his head couldn't be ignored. Iktomi slapped his head as his mind whispered, "Now you can't trick this giant. You've told him who you are."

Troll smiled. Now he understood what this small being was. "You are like our *nøkk*."

"No — what?" Iktomi asked.

"Nøkk," repeated Troll. "In Norway a nøkk enjoys having fun with humans. He plays tricks on them and teases them. Sometimes it is fun; sometimes his tricks are cruel."

Iktomi was speechless. "Hmm," he mumbled. "Perhaps your nøkk and I have like manners. But," he protested, "I am never cruel." He changed the subject. "Where is Norway?"

Troll, too, was without words; his heart ached with homesickness and his tears spilled. "Norway is far — far from this place," he sobbed. Now the words came as fast as his tears. "My home was on the loveliest mountain in all of Norway. On it are tall dark pines through which gentle breezes hum ancient songs in the long summer twilight. There is a cold, sweet stream leaping down the

18

mountain until it flows into the fjord. The waters of the fjord are deep blue and—," Troll couldn't go on; his shoulders heaved with sobs.

Iktomi looked away from the weeping giant, not to be polite, as the Lakota are, but because he was embarrassed that he did not know what Troll was talking about. Iktomi had often boasted of his wide travels, but he'd never been to such a place as the giant described.

"How does one get to Norway?"

Troll shook his head, spattering salty tears over the fire. "I don't know. I am lost."

"Well," Iktomi was disgusted with the weeping giant. "How did you get here?"

Troll wiped his tears away, cleared his throat, and began his tale.

FIVE

Mother Said, "Go"

Troll's seat on the boulder at the entrance to his cave was still lit by the midsummer sun, but the house was shadowed by his mountain. As old as Norway, Troll was usually comfortable on the rock he had sat on for so many centuries that it was polished and worn to fit his stout frame. But now he shifted and squirmed; he was uneasy because he saw lamplight flickering in the window of the farmhouse below his cave.

"Why are they still awake?" Troll sighed. A gentle breeze stirred the pines above the house. "What is causing such activity in my humans' house? It is so late. Is someone ill?"

Troll had always been able to tell what was going to happen to his humans, but now he was confused. For several weeks he had sensed excitement in the family. Mette, the mother, bustled about in a frenzy of washing and ironing and patching and mending clothes for the boy Olaf, her youngest son. But also she helped Oline, the wife of her oldest son, Thor, with her laundry and sewing.

20

Oline still rose in the early morning to milk the two cows and take them to pasture, but now she rushed home to skim the cream, churn the butter, and bake bread. Troll was amazed to see Thor help his wife with her chores so that he could cart the surplus milk, cream, butter, and bread to town to sell for money.

Troll did not understand money or why it was suddenly needed. The men wanted it so much that not only Thor but Svend and Olaf made daily trips down the mountain to get it. Troll watched them stride vigorously away in the morning and plod wearily up the mountain in the evening with heads bowed in exhaustion.

Troll, his curiosity aroused, had followed Svend and his sons down the mountain, through the valley, and around another mountain until they reached the city. Troll had never been in such a busy place, but he followed the men as they went from building to building, asking strange men for work. "Perhaps I can help them," he thought, despite his unease in the traffic, noise, and crowds of the city. But when they did find work, each was sent off in a different direction and Troll did not know whom to follow. Sadly, he returned to his mountain. "I can't help my humans in such a place—too many people, too many buildings." Troll had not liked the city.

"Why," Troll wondered, "do they need money so badly that they leave the farm to labor in the city?"

He was worried, and he did not like the feeling. He yawned and sighed as the mountain's shadow reached his rock. He thought about going into the cave to sleep, but there was still a light in the farmhouse, and he would not retire until the family did.

"What are they doing?"

Troll jumped when he heard the question, which was a spoken echo of his concern. His eyes strained through the gathering dusk and saw Nisse perched on the sod roof of the *stabbur*.

Usually Troll and Nisse ignored each other. The last time they had spoken was over four hundred years ago when neither could understand why the humans were dying.

"You live closer to the house," Troll said to Nisse. "Don't you know?"

"I'm not sure. I heard Thor and Olaf say they had been to the priest for a pass to leave the district, but I don't know where they want to go." Nisse shook his head.

"It must be a sad place," he went on. "This morning Oline wept the whole time she milked the cows. My bowl of cream was salty."

"Does Mette weep?" Troll asked, thinking of another mother of centuries past who cried for her sick and dying children.

"No," Nisse replied. "But she storms about giving orders as if there is much to be done, and she slams the lids on the kettles."

Troll was more puzzled by Nisse's report. The two stared silently at the light in the farmhouse. "I think I saw a tear on Svend's face," Nisse softly said.

Troll jumped up from his boulder at the outrageous statement. "Svend has never wept!"

"He did today. Right here," Nisse pointed down to the *stabbur* roof. "He looked at the few sacks of grain, and I saw a tear."

22

Troll was shocked. He stared at the house. The window was dark. Nisse stood, stretched, and clambered down the *stabbur* roof. "I don't believe it!" Troll called after Nisse, who didn't respond as he trotted toward the barn and his bed in the hay.

Troll was too weary to think any more about Svend weeping. Darkness flowed over the valley; Troll turned into his cave. Now that his humans were abed, he could sleep.

But it was a brief nap in the short hours of the summer night. "Whaa—?" Troll called, not sure what had roused him. He scrambled out of the cave and his mouth froze in a wide yawn at what he saw below.

Mette was embracing Oline, who was clad in her usual work bunad but now had her church shawl about her shoulders in the chill, damp dawn. More startling was the sight of Svend embracing his sons and wiping tears from his eyes. He moved to his wife's side and put his arm about the sobbing woman's shoulders. They stood close, holding each other, and watched the young people walk down the mountain.

Thor held Oline's hand even though he was burdened with a pack on his back and carried a bulky bundle in the other hand. Oline toted a smaller bundle. Olaf pushed a cart piled high with Oline's dowry trunk, several bags, and packs. Olaf stumbled and staggered to keep the cart from hurtling down the steep path. Thor released Oline's hand, grabbed the cart handle, and helped Olaf guide it to the gate. The three turned and looked up at the farm and the old couple standing forlornly in the yard. Quietly, the family gazed at each other. Troll found himself whispering, "Come back."

Slowly Thor raised his arm to his parents, then held the gate open for Oline who called "Farewell!" Her voice was choked with tears. Olaf hesitated longer, taking a step back up the path. "Olaf!" Thor commanded. The boy gave one last look, lifted his cap to his parents, and pushed the cart through the gate. Thor latched it and, without looking back, led the way to the road.

"Oline didn't milk the cows," grumbled Nisse from the *stabbur* roof. "She didn't leave me my bowl of cream."

"Quiet!" growled Troll. He didn't have time for Nisse's complaining, for his heart ached for Svend and Mette, who stood and wept in each other's arms. Svend stood back, patted Mette's shoulder, picked up the milk buckets, and went to the barn.

"Svend is going to milk!" exclaimed Nisse, and he vaulted from the *stabbur* to the barn.

"What has happened?" Troll was even more confused. A Norwegian farmer rarely milked the cows.

Troll shook his head. He was stunned at all he had seen. He turned to the comfort of his cave, but another shock stopped him. Mette stood at the cave's mouth. She could not see Troll but she knew he was near. Troll cringed, desperately looking at the sky, the mountains, the valley—everywhere but directly at Mette. He knew in his heart that she would ask something of him, and he did not want to hear what she wanted. Only once before in his memory had a human mother asked for help. Four hundred years ago, another woman had begged him to help save her sick and

24

dying children. He had been helpless then, and perhaps he would be so now—if he listened to Mette's request.

"Troll," Mette summoned, her voice choked with grief. Despite his desire to avoid looking into her eyes, Troll had to obey this mother and listen to her plea.

"Troll," Mette said again. The damp grass stirred beneath Troll's reluctant sigh. He gazed at the woman, who gave him a sad smile. Now she could see him, and he was trapped.

"Troll," she wept. "I need you. Did you see my Thor and Oline leave? And Olaf—" she faltered. Troll's eyes filled with tears. "They are going to America. Far across the ocean. This farm is not large enough for them and Svend and me to live on—" Troll heard her sobs and felt the despair of the mother's heart. "They will never return."

Troll was shocked. "Leaving the farm? Leaving Norway? Never return?" he muttered. Only the Vikings had ever left Norway, and most of them had returned.

"Troll, go with them," Mette begged.

"NO!" Troll roared. His deep protest thundered across the valley and boomed over the mountains. Mette paled and clenched her hands tightly, but she stood firm.

Troll's roar rumbled to silence and Mette's quiet voice pierced his ancient heart.

"Please."

Troll slumped on his worn boulder; he put his hands over his ears to shut out the mother's voice, but he could not.

"I am afraid for Thor and his young wife—and for Olaf,"

Mette went on. "They are going to a strange land—so far away. I am afraid that they will forget. . . ." Her hand moved to encompass the farm, the valley, the mountain. "Here, you and Nisse help us. In that new world, they will be alone."

"Are there no trolls in that new place?" Troll interrupted.

"I don't think so," Mette said. "I think there are only Indians there."

"Indians?" Troll asked. "Are they like trolls?"

Mette shook her head. "No, I believe they are human but have red skins."

Troll shivered at the vision of humans with scarlet bodies. "NO!" he said again.

"Yes," Mette said firmly. "You must go with them. Here in Norway even trolls are in danger. They have increased in number, as have the people. Some of the people must go to America to feed themselves and some of the trolls must go, too.

"You must go to protect and help, as you do here. If you are with them, the children will not forget their homes."

"Why can't Nisse go?" Troll asked. He heard the frightened chatter of Nisse listening from the *stabbur*.

"We need Nisse here. Svend is old and needs all the good luck that Nisse can bring to the farm. His power can only work on a farm, and the children will not have a farm in America for some time. But you—your powers can be used anywhere. You are strong and can help Thor and Olaf build their new farm. Oline will need your help caring for the children she will have. It will be

26

as it has been here," Mette persuaded. "You will help a mother in the new world just as you have helped mothers in this place. You will take a part of Norway to America."

Troll couldn't help but be pleased with Mette's confidence in his powers. He would have to go to this new world — this America. He sighed and stood. "If I don't like this new land, I will come back."

Mette nodded but lowered her head so that Troll could not see her sad smile and the tears that flowed again. "Thank you," she whispered.

Troll started down the mountain. With a few giant steps he could catch up to the emigrants, but he dawdled. He opened the gate, turned, and looked back at the house, barn, and *stabbur*. Nisse, perched in his usual place, waved his red hat. Mette stood in front of the house, and Svend joined her. Troll willed himself visible, and the man and woman waved. Troll shut the gate and walked to the road.

Striding through the valley, Troll gazed up at the pine-clad mountains rising to towering, jagged peaks. Tears filled his eyes at the beauty around him. His heart throbbed "Farewell!" to the trees, the mountains, and the little stream that leapt and tumbled down the mountain until it gurgled under the narrow bridge in the valley. Boisterous laughter greeted Troll as he paused on the bridge to take one last look at the valley and his mountain.

"Where do you think you are going?" bubbled a voice. Troll recognized the nøkk of the stream.

"To America," Troll answered, and he strode across the bridge. He didn't trust Nøkk, who liked to play tricks on those who used the bridge.

Nøkk's laughter followed him, and Troll thought he heard "Foolish troll!" gurgling in the tumbling stream.

The trail narrowed into a curve, then straightened at the cross-roads. A beautiful young woman suddenly appeared in the middle of the road. Enticingly, she smiled at Troll.

"Oh, just a troll," she complained as she recognized the approaching being. Before Troll's eyes she became an ugly old woman.

"Don't bother me, Hulder," Troll said, avoiding the creature's eyes.

"Hmph!" The hulder disgustedly switched her cow's tail. "Where do you think you are going, Troll?"

"I am going with my humans to America," Troll said, and he looked both ways at the fork in the road, not sure which way to go.

"I suppose you mean that ignorant young man and clumsy boy who paid no attention to me because of the weeping girl." The hulder pointed to the left.

"Wait," the hulder called as Troll walked away. He turned and she was again a lovely young woman. "Why don't you stay with me, Troll? So many young men are leaving Norway, I'll settle for you."

But Troll, immune to the hulder's magic, kept walking. "Fool!" growled the hulder.

Troll lengthened his stride. He didn't want to meet any more nøkks or hulders, or even another troll. Soon he had caught up with Thor, Oline, and Olaf. He walked alongside, then sat on the cart Olaf pushed. If he had to leave Norway, Troll decided, he would not tire himself walking.

Olaf immediately began to strain and groan. "This cart is getting heavier. What have you packed in it, Oline?"

"Only those things I will need to keep house in America," Oline's already red and swollen eyes flooded with tears. "The things my mother gave me when I was married," she sobbed. Angrily she turned to Thor. "If my parents had known that only a few months after our wedding you would be taking me to a strange land, they would never have given their consent!"

Thor sighed, and Troll knew that the young man had heard this complaint before. "It is the only way," he said patiently. "You know my father's farm cannot support us, nor will we ever have our own land in Norway. In America we will have a farm on three, four times as much land—just you and me. Even Olaf can have his own farm. We will be rich in America. Here we would always be poor—if we did not starve to death."

"Thor," groaned Olaf, "I must rest. The cart is so heavy. If only our troll were here to help push."

Invisibly, Troll jumped to the ground. He was disgusted. "Why did the boy have to say that?" Now Troll would have to walk and help push. He took one side of the cart's handle.

"Why," Olaf exclaimed, "the cart is much lighter now!"

"Perhaps Troll *is* with us," Oline said, and she looked about.

"Nonsense," Thor said. "Trolls don't leave Norway—if there really are trolls. Such myths are part of the past. We are going to everything new!"

"Why didn't I think to tell Mette that," Troll wished.

The three humans, the invisible Troll beside them, walked until the sun was high and they reached the fjord. "Let us rest and have our lunch while we wait for the ferry." Thor sat on a bench near the ferry landing.

Troll's mouth watered as Oline unwrapped the buttered bread and cheese that Mette had sent with them. He could go for long periods without food, but through the ages he had become accustomed to the food human mothers had left at his cave. "I must forget eating," Troll said, and he looked away.

He gazed at the mountain lake, its water as blue as the cloudless sky, mirroring the mountains in its still depths. "Ohh," Troll groaned, suddenly realizing that not only were he and his humans going to cross the fjord in a boat, but they would also cross the ocean in one. Foreboding filled his heart.

SIX

America

Troll's shoulders shook with deep sobs. His huge hand swiped at his eyes and nose until his weeping turned to sighs.

Iktomi said nothing. He averted his gaze from Troll and tossed dry sticks into the dying fire. He was trying to be polite in the presence of such noisy grief, but he grew impatient with Troll's shuddering sighs.

"What next?" Iktomi asked. "How did you get here?"

Troll took a deep breath, wiped his eyes again, and continued his story. "We crossed the fjord on a ferryboat. Or my humans did. I tried to sit with them, but the water seeped over the sides."

"The boat's sinking!" screamed Oline.

Troll knew that even though he couldn't be seen, his great weight was swamping the ferry. He eased himself into the icy fjord. He sank down, down until the water was over his head. He held his breath and plodded through the fjord. The water was so

31

clear that he had no trouble seeing the ferry above him. Soon his head emerged and he gratefully drew a breath. He shivered and shook the water from his body, spattering the humans in the ferry.

"Is it raining?" Olaf looked up at the clear sky.

"No," Thor answered gruffly. "Come on, help pull the cart off of the ferry. We have a long walk ahead."

They walked for two more days. The humans trudged silently, but Troll was glad that Oline had stopped weeping.

At sundown the second day, they pulled the cart off the road. Thor pulled blankets from the trunk while Oline set out the cold supper. Troll's stomach rumbled when he saw the food, but he walked away to find a sun-warmed rock and settled next to it. The weary humans wrapped themselves in the blankets and slept by the cart.

The short Norwegian night quickly ended and Troll awoke to bright sun already drying his dewy shirt. His humans were packing the blankets away. They pushed the cart back on the road and began their final day in Norway.

("We came to a great city," Troll told Iktomi, who still couldn't imagine what a city was. "Thor led us to the water and told us to wait while he went for the tickets.")

Oline began to weep again. "Oh, where is Thor? He's been gone so long."

"He'll be back. Don't worry, Oline," Olaf comforted.

Troll hoped that perhaps Thor couldn't get the tickets and they'd have to return to the farm. But Thor came running. "I have them!" he shouted, his face flushed with excitement. "Come," he ignored Oline's tears. "We must hurry to the pier to our ship. We must board her tonight. She embarks at dawn!"

Troll followed the humans through the crowded docks. Troll's nostrils quivered at the unfamiliar fishy odor that filled the damp air.

They had to leave the cart on the dock. Thor found a fisherman who bought it. "Too cheap," Thor grumbled, but he pocketed the coins. He knew they'd need money in America.

Troll couldn't help Olaf and Thor with the heavy trunk as they eased it down two steep stairways. An official checked their tickets and pointed toward a dark, damp hold.

Troll held his breath. The place reeked of too many humans crammed into a small space. Not only was it smelly, but it buzzed and roared with the chatter of the men and women and the cries of children.

Troll watched his humans find their space, but he could not follow. His skin crawled, his heart raced in panic. He could not stay in this dark, crowded, stinking hole. He made his way to the upper deck. His humans could stay in that terrible place, but if he, Troll, had to go to America, he would do so in the open.

"Ahh, it was bad," Troll whispered, and Iktomi had to lean closer to hear. "Days and nights — so many I lost count. The ship rolled and pitched through giant waves, and my humans got sick.

"And the storms! I, who have lived through hundreds of mountain winters, thought I would die on the ocean!" Troll moaned in remembered agony.

"Ocean?" Iktomi asked. "What is that?"

Troll waved his hand over and beyond the lake. "It is like this pond with no shore—only water reaching as far as one can see. . . . That is the ocean! Water so vast I feared I would never see land again!"

Iktomi's eyes popped wide, his mouth gaped, and his mind went blank. No part of Iktomi could comprehend so much water.

"At last," Troll went on, "the voyage ended. We docked at a city larger than the one we had left in Norway. Noise, people everywhere. . . . We had to struggle to make our way through the packed streets. I had to shove people out of my humans' way. Then we came to this—this immense iron monster." Troll shuddered at the recollection. "It was roaring and belching fire and smoke."

"What?" Iktomi cried in disbelief.

"Yah," nodded Troll. "And behind the monster were wagons— like houses on wheels—all hooked together. My humans and I climbed into one; the monster screamed, bells rang. The roar grew into a rushing rumble and the wagon jerked ahead. We were thrown about on hard wooden seats. Then the roar and rumble settled into a clackity, clackity rhythm. We saw the city rush by the windows and soon there were fields with cattle. Trees flew past, we went above a river, then there were towns and more fields. . . . We traveled across America in this monster my humans called a train."

"Go on," Iktomi urged, fascinated by Troll's story and irritated by the giant's pause.

"We slept on the train. My humans bought food at the places the train stopped. At last, in a place called Wisconsin, my humans and I left the train.

"It was a lovely country—green, wooded—that reminded my humans of Norway. But there were no mountains.

"My humans found Uncle Karl, one of Mette's brothers who had left Norway many years ago. He allowed my humans to live with him and his wife for the winter. He helped Thor get work at a sawmill and found a job for Olaf chopping wood for the village shops. Oline helped with the household chores and didn't seem to mind the stay, but for Olaf and Thor it was a long winter.

"They had to work to save money for the journey that would resume when spring came. When the weather warmed, they had enough funds to buy a team of oxen and a wagon. They also bought a plow, a cow, chickens, seeds for planting, and food for the journey. The wagon was so loaded that there was barely room for Oline's trunk.

"Thor had never driven oxen before. He sat on the high wagon seat; he whistled and slapped the reins, but the beasts didn't move. Olaf cracked a whip over their heads and rumps, but they still didn't move. Troll grabbed the yoke and pulled. The oxen took a step and then stopped. Thor yelled, Olaf whipped, and Oline cried. Uncle Karl was no help—he had no experience with oxen.

"At last an American told Thor the English words to persuade the oxen to move. Thor shouted the commands and slapped the reins on their rumps, and the beasts plodded ahead.

"My humans were pleased, but they didn't see the American laughing at Thor," Troll sadly recalled. "The American had given Thor English words that were profane curses, but they always made the oxen move.

"Again we traveled—many days and nights, through bright, warm days and gray, rainy days. My humans camped each night near a lake or stream, sleeping under the wagon on the ground. I watched over them as they slept and made sure the oxen did not stray.

"At first the land was good. Hills, lakes, trees—land that reminded us of Norway. But the land was all claimed—other humans farmed there—so we went on.

"At a wide river, Thor shouted the English words, but the oxen would not move because they were afraid of the ferry. I pulled the oxen onto the ferry.

"I had hoped the journey would end after the river crossing. We were all weary, but we kept on, fording many small streams. We came to where trees no longer grew and the land rose in rolling swells that reminded me of the ocean, but there was no water."

Troll stared into the fire.

Iktomi cleared his throat, waiting for Troll to continue, but the giant sat silent until Iktomi asked, "What then?"

Tears were again on Troll's face as he shook his head. "I don't know. I was following the wagon and I stepped on a spiny plant. I stopped to pull out a thorn stuck in my foot. When I started to walk—they were gone."

"Gone?" Iktomi stormed. "Gone where?"

"I don't know," Troll mourned. "Just gone, as if the earth had opened up and swallowed them."

"So," Iktomi urged the giant, who was weeping again. "What did you do?"

"I walked—walked and walked for days and days—looking for my humans. I knew I was lost. I was weary and so thirsty—all I thought of was water. Then I looked down and saw an eye peering up out of the grass."

The sun was a red ball that seemed to rest on the lake's calm surface. Its rays shimmered in violet trails that reached the shore where Iktomi and Troll sat, unheeding of the beauty of the sunset.

Iktomi's whole being pondered the tale Troll had told. The trickster had been on long treks alone or with the Lakota and had seen many new and strange sights. He had followed them to Paha Sapa, their sacred mountains, where they had worshipped the Great Spirit and cut lodge poles. But Iktomi had never crossed an ocean, nor had he seen a city nor ridden on an iron monster. His head shook with wonder at all Troll had told.

Troll sighed, stirring the glowing embers of the fire into flame. He yawned, making ashes fluff into the air. Weary, so weary, Troll stretched his great body on the sand and slept.

Iktomi shivered from the cool breeze blowing across the lake. He curled into a tight ball on the sand near the fire. Yawning, he closed his eyes, but the night wind chilled his back. Iktomi turned his back to the fire, but now his front was cold.

"Oh for a warm teepee and soft buffalo robe," he grumbled and rolled over. Glancing at the giant who slept despite the cool night, Iktomi's sleepy mind sent him a message. Quickly, Iktomi crawled into the space between Troll and the fire, wiggled into a warm spot in the sand, and slept.

SEVEN

Looking for the Lost Humans

Å kjøre vatten, å kjøre ve',
å kjøre tømmer over heia.

Iktomi's ears twitched; one eye and then the other opened. "Whaa—?" the trickster mumbled. He sat up, confused by a booming bass voice singing strange words to a lilting air. Then Iktomi understood.

"I carry water, I carry wood," Troll sang and splashed in the lake. Iktomi saw the giant's garments dripping from branches high in a tree. Iktomi stood and stretched, and Troll sang, "I carry lumber from the val-ley."

Troll ducked, and bubbles rose as he continued singing under water. Iktomi stared, waiting and waiting for Troll to emerge. He took a step toward the lake to see if Troll was still there.

"Blll-aaahhhh!" Troll emerged, blowing, sputtering, and spattering blobs of water.

Iktomi stared at the giant's naked body. Troll was big with his clothes on, but Iktomi's eyes could not believe what they saw. Muscles knotted Troll's arms, rippled strongly in his back, and bulged in thighs that were bigger than many of the tree trunks around the lake.

Iktomi backed away from the lake; Troll was making huge waves as he splashed to shore. Troll's body sparkled with rainbow glints from the water clinging to the hair on his chest, arms, and legs. Never had Iktomi seen such a hairy two-legged creature—other than a bear.

"Are your humans like you?" Iktomi asked.

Troll shook his head and glittering drops spattered Iktomi. "They are much smaller."

"No, no," Iktomi moved away from Troll's spray. "Are they covered with hair the way you are?"

Troll looked down at his nakedness and nodded. "The men are," he explained. He wrung water from his beard. "But not the women and children."

"Are they as white as—" Iktomi pointed to Troll's bare belly. The giant's skin, usually covered with clothing, was pasty white compared to his sunburned face, forearms, and hands.

Troll looked at his stomach. "Yah." He combed his beard with his fingers and a fish flopped out of the matted hair and landed at Iktomi's feet.

Troll and Iktomi stared at the gasping fish, then Iktomi pounced on it before it could flop back into the water.

"Go!" Iktomi yelled, "Catch more fish! Your beard is a fine net."

"*Nei,*" Troll refused. "I have had my bath and am almost dry — oh, here's another."

Iktomi laughed and grabbed the second fish. He looked about for wood to add to the fire. He cleaned the fish, saying, "These will do for me, but you will go hungry if you don't catch more for yourself." He recalled Troll's appetite of the night before.

"No matter," Troll said. "I found some duck eggs and ate some berries before you awoke."

Iktomi paused in his breakfast preparation to glare at Troll. "Why didn't you wake me?" he demanded. He almost fell into the fire when Troll's deep-throated chuckles set the treetops shaking.

"HO, HO, HO," Troll laughed, reaching for the fish. "Are you going to share with me?" He chortled more as Iktomi hugged the fish to his chest. "Never mind, little one," Troll said. "I don't want your fish."

Iktomi was dismayed at how the giant's mood had changed from the night before. Then he was a sad, helpless, pitiful being. But this morning he seemed cheerfully confident, as if he had regained pride in himself. Last night Iktomi thought that he could easily have persuaded Troll to do what he wanted him to, but not now. Now, Iktomi admitted, Troll was someone to fear.

Iktomi's legs quivered when he walked to the water. His hands trembled when he washed the fish. He found some green twigs to skewer the fish over the fire and did not look at Troll until he had eaten.

When his stomach was fully content, Iktomi leaned against the tree and watched Troll explore the beach and shoreline. "Singing again," Iktomi thought, "if that's what that noise is called."

"Ho!" Iktomi rose. "I want no more of the ugly one's company." He urged his feet to walk away from the lake before Troll noticed his going.

But Troll saw Iktomi dart into the trees. He kept singing as he took one long stride to Iktomi's side.

Iktomi's feet skittered away. "Go away!" Iktomi tried to keep his voice from trembling. "I have important duties to attend to and I don't want you following along!" He turned his back on the giant, but his feet only strode through air.

"Aagh," Iktomi squealed as the giant's hands squeezed about his waist.

"Put me down!" Iktomi screamed, anger replacing his fear. He pounded on Troll's nose.

Hør det kaller, hør det lokker, Troll sang, holding the kicking, hitting, and yelling Iktomi at arm's length. "Hear the voice of nature calling," Troll's deep bass boomed over Iktomi's angry yells.

Finally, exhausted, Iktomi ceased his struggles. "Ho, ugly one," he sighed, "I surrender."

Troll smiled and nodded. "I'm glad that you are sensible. You know this barbarous land and all the creatures in it. You will help me find my humans."

"What!" Iktomi screamed in protest, but he felt the giant's hand tighten. "How can I?" he whined. "This land is big—vast as your ocean. It will take forever to find your humans."

"We have time," Troll smiled.

"But I don't know where to start," Iktomi protested, his mind busily thinking of excuses.

"Do you remember where I found you?" Troll asked.

"Where *I* found *you*," Iktomi corrected. "You were the lost one. Yes, I know the place."

"That's where we will start," Troll said. "And," he went on, his deep voice gently persuasive, "I once heard humans speaking of your kind. They said Indians could find the smallest sign to follow animals—or humans. Is this true?"

Iktomi nodded, warily watching the giant.

"Then you," Troll smiled, "the wise one of the Lakota, must surely be more skilled than your people. I know that you will easily find my humans' trail."

"Well," Iktomi tried to be modest, "I have followed many trails."

Troll smiled to himself, thinking, "As I thought, this one is a vain creature." But aloud he said, "I knew it! You are indeed the wisest of all! And because wise beings are always kind and merciful, I know you will help me."

Iktomi, flattered by Troll's words, agreed as though he had never thought of objecting to the quest. He patted Troll's hands about his middle. "Now, please put me down."

43

"Of course, friend," Troll said. Then to further encourage Iktomi to stay, he added, "Tonight, if we again camp by a lake, I will catch fish for you."

And so the two ageless beings became traveling companions. They came to know each other well in the many days they were together.

Iktomi was dismayed when Troll began every day with a song. Usually Iktomi understood the words Troll sang, even in Norwegian, of the sun, dancing water, and pretty girls. But when Troll sang of an old woman "with a cane milking a cow, eight quarts sour cream, four half pounds of butter," Iktomi was confused.

"What is cow? What is quarts sour cream? What is pounds butter?" Iktomi asked grouchily, and he was amazed at the way Troll seemed to glory in explaining Norwegian dairy delights as he remembered them.

"A cow is a most wonderful animal — docile, tame. Ours let Mother take her milk into a wooden bucket." Troll closed his eyes and sniffed, remembering the warm, sweet odor that rose from the full bucket. "Then she poured it into a pan to cool and let the cream rise — mmm." Troll licked his lips. "The sweet cream was used to make *rømmegrøt,* and she always left a full bowl at my cave." Troll's eyes rolled in ecstasy. "And butter. She made butter and cheese and —"

"Enough!" Iktomi yelled. "Don't tell me any more of such disgusting — I've never heard of these things!"

Troll looked at Iktomi and a tear slid into his beard. "Aahh."

He breathed a sad sigh and fell silent. He had almost tasted the sweetness of it all, but now he wondered if he ever would again.

Troll plodded along, but the brightness of the day and the song of birds flying from the grass at his feet soon dispelled his gloom. His deep voice broke into his favorite song, "I carry water, I carry wood," which Iktomi had come to know as well as Troll did.

"Oh, no." Iktomi's ears tried not to listen, and his mind furiously thought of ways to end Troll's ceaseless concert.

"Hmph," Iktomi politely cleared his throat, but Troll was too engrossed in his song to hear. "HMMPH!" Iktomi was not so polite this time, and Troll's song faded and he looked questioningly at Iktomi.

"Your songs, O Great One," Iktomi fawned, "are unknown in this land—not that they are not pleasing to hear—" he quickly added when Troll frowned. "But they are strange— new—and may offend the little people of the prairie."

Troll looked at the waves of grass flowing in all directions. "Little people?" he asked. "Like you?"

"Not in size," replied Iktomi. "They are smaller—but, yes, they are like me in that we both have special gifts. But the little people live below and take care of the prairie. One must be careful not to offend any of them."

"Why?" Troll wanted to know. "What can these little people do?"

"They can cause misfortune of—of all sorts," Iktomi impatiently explained, appalled at the giant's ignorance. "If the little people don't like your songs, they may make it difficult — maybe impossible — to find the trail left by your humans."

Iktomi saw Troll flinch in alarm. Iktomi shrugged. "But if you'd rather sing . . . ?"

"I will not," Troll said. "I must find my humans. I will not risk offending anyone." Warily he looked around as if he might spot a small person watching.

As the two resumed their trek, Troll was quiet, but once in a while he forgot and hummed the melody to "I carry water." Iktomi would glare, and Troll would stop.

As the days progressed, the melodies that filled Troll's head became increasingly melancholy, until by evening he was humming dirges while tears flowed and he had to blow his nose. "I must find my humans," he would sob until Iktomi, exasperated by the mournful Troll, would angrily retort, "We will, if you shut up!"

So the marches were silent, save for the thud of Troll's steps muffled in the tall grass. "Oh, where are my humans?" he cried to himself.

Troll had not questioned Iktomi's tracking skill after the trickster had backtracked Troll's trail to where the humans had disappeared. Iktomi had quickly found broken, dried grass that had been crushed by the immigrants' heavy wagon. Troll would not have seen the sign, nor would he have found oxen spoor along the way without Iktomi's help. So he believed Iktomi was leading him to the humans.

"But," thought Troll, "the wagon moves slowly — we should

46

have found it by now." But he did not let Iktomi know of his doubts.

As the pair followed the faint trail they sighted deer, antelope, and once, to Iktomi's great excitement, a buffalo.

"Go!" Iktomi yelled at Troll. "You can catch it with your giant strides. GO!"

"*Nei,*" Troll shook his head.

"Yes, you can," Iktomi tried flattery. "You can move more swiftly than the wind. Your hands are quick, nimble, and strong. You could easily kill—and then we would have meat." Iktomi's stomach rumbled in anticipation.

"*Nei,*" Troll repeated, and Iktomi flew into a stomping rage, but when they next spotted a deer he did not say anything to Troll. He didn't want to be squeezed in the giant's hands.

Iktomi tried to satisfy his hunger with the buffalo berries that abundantly filled the draw where they spent a night. The next morning he awoke to Troll's "carry water" song. "OHH," Iktomi groaned, "I wish I had never found this giant!" Still he rose, and, grumbling, he scanned the area until he found the immigrants' trail and sullenly followed it.

Troll muffled his song to a buzzing hum and trod after Iktomi, who hissed, "Quiet!" and pointed at a herd of antelope calmly grazing in the morning-damp grass. Too late! The antelope lifted their heads for only a second before they sped in panicky flight.

"Dolt!" stormed Iktomi. "I was almost close enough to kill one. If you won't hunt, let me. Don't frighten game away!" He turned and watched the fleeing antelope. Unbelieving, he saw one stumble and fall, its slender leg snapped in a prairie-dog hole.

"Ho, *waste!*" shouted Iktomi, and he ran to the downed creature. Its eyes rolled and it struggled to rise.

"Now," exulted Iktomi, "we will have meat!" But when he reached the antelope he stopped, frustrated. He had no knife. "Poor creature," Troll pitied, and his great hands reached down to end its misery. Tears dripped from his nose because of what he had to do, but he could not let the small beast suffer.

He hoisted the carcass to his shoulder and carried it to the evening's camp. Quietly he helped Iktomi dress it, quartering it with his hands while Iktomi gathered buffalo chips for a fire.

The two spent most of the afternoon roasting and eating the meat. "Hmm," Iktomi patted his full stomach, whose need for meat was satisfied. "Wasn't that delicious?"

Troll nodded, reluctantly admitting that he had relished the meal.

"Now, perhaps you will hunt for more game?"

"No," Troll was adamant. "I only killed this beast to end its suffering. I will not deliberately harm another."

Iktomi was again exasperated with the giant, but he said nothing as they prepared for sleep.

EIGHT

The Trail Is Lost

Iktomi slept soundly under the stunted tree where he and Troll camped, but a thundering crash roused him. His eyes opened to bright flashes quickly followed by another boom. In the sharp light he saw Troll standing, arms raised to the thunderstorm.

"*Witco!* Fool!" yelled Iktomi, and he rolled away from the tree. "Get down!" he ordered Troll.

But the giant did not heed him. "Look!" he cried. "It is Thor's hammer pounding and sending sparks from heaven." He cowered as he felt the hair on the back of his neck and his arms rise.

Iktomi felt it too. He jumped up and ran full tilt into Troll, knocking the giant off balance so that he staggered and fell. Iktomi rolled away and put his arms over his head. A thunderbolt rushed down to the earth. The stunted tree glowed before it exploded into fiery flames, sending sparks into the dry grass. But the fires were doused in the torrent that followed the thundering blast.

Iktomi and Troll were soon cold and shivering in the drenching rain. Then they cowered with their heads down and arms raised against stinging pellets of hail that turned to larger balls. Iktomi cried out in pain.

Troll rolled to his stomach and pressed his face into the wet grass to protect his eyes. "Ice stones?" he wondered. Never had he seen such a ferocious storm.

Soon the icy pelting ceased and the rain became gentle drops. The lightning flashes moved to the east, and the thunder became dull echoes. Iktomi looked up to see stars breaking through the dark clouds. He rose and walked to the downed tree. He found a branch and poked at the steaming trunk. "Good," he muttered as he found glowing embers. He held his hands to their warmth, then curled up as near as he could and went back to sleep.

But Troll lay stunned and wetly miserable. "What a terrible land," he moaned. He envied Iktomi's ability to sleep, for Troll didn't think he could rest. But his weariness won and his snores soon echoed the distant thunder.

In the morning all was sunshine. The pair rose and plodded along, Iktomi grumbling in his mind because his stomach was empty and complaining again.

"Last night was terrible," Troll said to Iktomi.

"It could have been worse," Iktomi growled. "Why were you standing up to reach for the thunderbolts?"

"I . . . I . . . ," Troll tried to find the words to explain the confusion he felt when he awoke to the lightning and thunder. "I thought I was home—in Norway. I thought it was the thunder god, Thor."

"Fool!" Iktomi had no sympathy. "Your god has no power over our Thunder Bird. You, with your arms raised, were highest thing on the prairie. If I hadn't knocked you down, you could have been killed."

Troll nodded sadly. "Perhaps it would have been better," he thought. "If I can't find my humans I will die anyway."

Iktomi walked away, then a thought came. "Wasn't Thor one of your humans?"

Troll nodded. "He was named for the god because Mette thought his first cries were as loud as thunder."

Iktomi had nothing to say, so the two marched quietly on. Iktomi's eyes searched for a sign of the wagon, and his mind worried because he couldn't find any. Then his mind had another idea.

"Great One," Iktomi addressed Troll, who glanced down at his companion without comment. The giant was no longer fooled by Iktomi's honeyed tones. "What does he want now?" Troll wondered.

"Great One," Iktomi went on, "in one stride you cover three times the distance that I do. And from your added height you can see much farther than I can. Could I—would you permit me to sit atop your strong shoulders? From there I can follow your humans' trail much better, and we can travel faster."

Troll was amused by Iktomi's attempts to cajole him into doing something the trickster wanted. But this suggestion made sense, and Troll's longing to find his humans was greater than ever.

So Troll agreed, because he needed Iktomi. Iktomi knew the land through which they traveled and where, alone, Troll could have been forever lost—or eventually would have died. For trolls could die when out of their natural homes, but more often they died of loneliness and heartbreak from lack of human companionship. Troll lifted Iktomi to his shoulders.

Iktomi was comfortable straddling Troll's neck, and his view *was* better. He carefully scanned the prairie around him. Iktomi was worried. He had not found the humans' trail. What would Troll do to him if he couldn't find his people?

But Iktomi also had another concern. In the several days he and the giant had traveled together, there had been no sign of the Lakota. Had Iktomi been alone, he would have searched for the tribe—for he too could not go long without companionship. Although being with Troll had met this need, the previous night's storm had made Iktomi long for the comfort and shelter of a teepee.

"Where are Troll's humans?" he wondered, but more importantly, "Where are my people?"

From the vantage of Troll's height, Iktomi's eyes restlessly scanned the plains. The signs of the wagon and oxen had been barely visible before the storm, but now they had vanished. Iktomi said nothing to Troll and kept to the direction they had followed the day before, hoping to find the trail again. Now the trickster also watched for signs of the Lakotas' passage — signs that might have been made by accident or that had been deliberately placed. But there was nothing.

Troll was anxious too. Even the bright sunshine did not cheer him as it usually did. He did not want to sing or speak. He had to force himself to move his feet in the direction Iktomi ordered. He was exhausted and so unhappy that tears clouded his eyes and he stumbled and nearly fell.

"Aaaiii!" Iktomi yelled, and he grabbed Troll's hair to keep from falling.

Troll paid no mind to his passenger. He carelessly plodded up a slight rise and looked up briefly only to see more grass before him. He gave a deep sigh, his rising shoulders jostling Iktomi.

"Careful, you—" Iktomi started to scold, but then he tugged Troll's matted hair and ordered, "Shh. Stop!"

Troll obeyed. A flicker of hope stirred in his heart. "What do you see?"

Iktomi didn't answer. His ears wiggled, trying to catch the faint sound they had heard — something vaguely familiar. Iktomi willed his whole body to listen, then he grabbed Troll's hair to keep from pitching to the ground.

Troll threw his head up and shouted with joy. He heard and recognized the sound Iktomi was trying to hear.

"It's Olaf!" he cried. He scanned the horizon, his eyes blinded with happy tears.

The light breeze faded and so did the sound, but it rose again with the wind. *Å kjøre vatten, å kjøre ve'*, Iktomi heard a boy's soprano trilling the song he'd come to detest.

"We've found them!" Troll exclaimed, and as he bounded forward Iktomi bounced off to the ground.

Iktomi lay moaning on the tough grass. Finally, he caught his breath and was able to rise. The giant was gone. "Good," he thought, "now we can search for the Lakota."

But Iktomi's mind was curious about Troll's humans. "Let us see what they look like." Iktomi followed Troll's trail.

At the top of the rise Iktomi paused, then lay prone on the grass to watch the scene below. He could not, as Troll did, will himself invisible, and he did not wish to be seen by Troll's humans until he studied them.

He watched a tall, lanky boy carry a bucket of water from the creek that flowed through a long valley. The boy gave the bucket to a woman waiting by the fire. Nearby was the wagon Iktomi had trailed. Some distance beyond he saw a man struggling to hold a plow in the tough sod as the oxen strained to pull it. Troll was at the man's side and his strong hands pushed the plow. The oxen jerked forward and the sod turned black under the man's feet.

"Bah!" Iktomi cried in disgust. "These humans are *wasicus*." He had seen others like them and was horrified as they tore Mother Earth's breast and built shelters. Then they claimed the land as theirs and forbade the Lakota passage through it.

"Let us go," his mind suggested, but his stomach rumbled, "I'm empty." That determined what Iktomi would do next.

He stood, patted his hair, and settled his head band. Holding himself proudly like a Lakota warrior, he walked to the wagon.

"*Hau, wiṅyan,*" he greeted Oline politely. Because he and Troll had spoken to each other, Iktomi had forgotten that this white woman would not understand him.

She turned, saw the lithe, dark, nearly naked figure, and screamed.

The boy, back at the creek, dropped the bucket and ran to the woman. The man let go of the plow and rushed toward Iktomi. But Troll reached Iktomi first.

"What have you done to Oline?" Troll growled.

Iktomi, startled at the humans' reaction and Troll's accusation, stood rigid, not daring to move. "I greeted the woman," he began to explain, then his eyes saw the man reaching for the rifle propped against the wagon wheel.

Iktomi quickly held up his hand in the peace sign, but the man leveled the rifle at him.

"What do you want?" the man demanded, but Iktomi did not understand.

"Troll," Iktomi called. "Don't let your man hurt me with that firestick!" He remembered another man who had pointed a rifle at him, and Iktomi's leg had caught an iron ball that burned. Even after it was removed, the wound had festered and pained him for a long time.

Troll put a finger on the rifle barrel, aiming it at the ground, and Thor could not lift it. "Go invisible," Troll urged Iktomi.

"I cannot!"

"Then leave," Troll said. "I cannot keep Thor from raising the rifle for very long."

Iktomi turned. His legs wanted to run, but the voice in his head commanded, "Walk bravely!" Iktomi stilled his trembling limbs and walked up the rise away from the wasicus.

Out of sight of the humans, Troll caught up with Iktomi. "I am sorry," he said. "You frightened Oline. Thor and Olaf thought you meant to harm her."

"Hah!" Iktomi spat. "What cowards your humans are. I would never harm such pitiful creatures! I only wanted something to eat before I went on my way."

"I know," Troll said, "but my humans have been told that your people will kill them."

The huge giant and the lithe trickster stared at each other; Iktomi in anger and Troll in sorrow. Iktomi turned and walked away.

"Farewell, friend," Troll softly called. "Thank you."

NINE

Where Are the Lakota?

Iktomi was going along, and he was hungry. He had made three camps since he had left Troll and had only berries to eat. He had not found the Lakota.

He had visited the old village sites along rivers and creeks but found only cold ashes of long-dead fires. Worse, he found more *wasicus* tearing up the earth. At first Iktomi hesitated to make contact with them after the unfriendly reception he'd had from Troll's humans. But his grumbling stomach overcame his reluctance.

"*Hau, kola,*" he said to a bearded man struggling with a plow and a team of horses. "Greetings, friend," Iktomi said in his best beguiling manner. "Welcome to Lakota land."

"What do you want?" the man growled, not even stopping his plowing.

Of course, Iktomi didn't understand the words, but he recognized the hostile tone. Then the man stopped, bent to pick up a clod of sod, and hurled it at Iktomi.

Iktomi ducked. The heavy clump sailed over his head and thunked on the ground behind him. "Get away from here," the white man ordered. "This is my land, and no   redskins better not   !"

Iktomi did not know the profanity the man used, but he understood that he was being cursed. He turned away.

Another night passed, and his stomach was not content with the raw *tipsila* Iktomi had resorted to digging. He followed what looked like a wagon trail and found more settlers. He decided to try one more time.

"*Hau*—," he began, but the man seated at the door of a sod house calmly lifted a rifle over his knees, its barrel aimed at Iktomi's empty stomach. "Git," the man said quietly, and again Iktomi turned away.

He wondered if these *wasicus* were really people. They were so unlike the Lakota. They were inhospitable and rude, whereas the Lakota welcomed travelers even if they were strangers and shared food and shelter without being asked.

"All these whites have driven the Lakota away," Iktomi's mind concluded. "Let us go west where there are fewer *wasicus*."

Iktomi's feet turned west toward the Minishosha, the great river. His people were probably hunting buffalo on the other side. Walking along the shore, he looked for signs of the Lakotas' crossing. He found none, and wearily he sat and drank from the sluggish stream. He lay back on the sand to rest awhile before resuming his quest.

High above him, he saw a dark speck circling as if it were touching the sky. Half asleep, Iktomi watched until his eyes recognized wambli, the eagle.

Iktomi watched the bird floating on the air currents. "Hunting," his mind decided as his eyes followed the graceful flight. Then his eyes moved to the high bluffs above the river. "Her nest must be up there." Iktomi sat up. "A nest, maybe eaglets—food." Iktomi got to his feet.

He started to climb the steep chalkstone bluff, his hands and feet finding holds in the rough surface. Now he could hear the screams of the hungry eaglets. He looked up to see how far he had to go and spotted the aerie in a stunted cedar. Iktomi rested; his knees, toes, and knuckles were scraped and stinging. His torso and thighs were white from rubbing against the chalky surface.

He looked down. "Ohh," he moaned as he suddenly realized how steep the bluff was and how high he was perched. "Don't slip," he cautioned his fingers and toes. He took a deep breath and climbed on.

At last, he grabbed a cedar root protruding from the cliff. He rested again and pulled himself up to peer into the nest.

Two eaglets were in the nest. When they saw Iktomi their cries turned to alarmed screeches. "They're not large enough to fly," Iktomi noted as he pulled himself into the nest. They retreated to one side, flapped their wings, and raised their small but sharp talons. Iktomi ignored them and hid himself in the refuse of the nest.

A shrill scream came down on the nest; the eaglets quieted and cowered. Large, dagger-sharp talons dug into Iktomi's shoulders and jerked him up.

"Owww!" Iktomi squealed in pain, but he could not pull out of the mother eagle's firm grasp. She flapped her wings and pulled him over the rim of the nest.

"Wait!" Iktomi cried to the enraged mother. "I mean no harm to your children! I only wanted a bit of their food!"

The eagle with withdrew her talons, leaving Iktomi dangling over the side of the nest. She fixed a fiery eye on Iktomi. "Get out, Trickster," she ordered, "before I pluck your nose for my children's feeding."

Quickly, Iktomi scrambled out of the nest. He grabbed the cedar to keep from plunging down to the river.

The eagle's eye never left him. "Shall I help you fly to the river?" she asked, raising her wings.

"No, Mother, no," Iktomi said calmly. His fear was gone, and his mind was rapidly sorting through methods of persuading the eagle to help him.

"Let me rest, Mother," he humbly begged. "I am weak with hunger. The steep climb . . . took . . . all . . . my . . . strength." His voice faded as if he were truly exhausted and faint.

Mother Eagle said nothing but kept her eye on Iktomi. The eaglets, too, were still.

Holding tightly to the branch, Iktomi weakly raised his head to look about. He was amazed at the view stretching out over the river and beyond.

"How fortunate you are, Mother, to have your nest in such a high place. You can see all the nations. You can look for food without moving from your home."

Mother Eagle stayed silent, but Iktomi was encouraged. She had lowered her wings.

"From this high place," he went on, "you can see the movements of the people." He paused and scanned the land below. Then with pretended surprise he said, "But, Mother, where are the Lakota?"

The eagle did not answer.

"Are they following the buffalo out of sight of this place?"

"Buffalo?" Iktomi jumped as the eagle squawked. Her eyes glared. "Hah! There are no buffalo!"

"What?" Iktomi did not believe this could be so. "How can that be? The Great Spirit gave the buffalo to the people to use forever."

Now the eagle turned her head to the right and then to the left as she viewed the prairie. "Where have you been, Iktomi? Haven't you heard the thunder from the many firesticks of the white hunters? Haven't you seen the smoke that rises when they shoot?"

Iktomi shook his head and grabbed for a better hold on the tree. "I know of firesticks," he replied, "but I did not know that they have destroyed all the buffalo."

"The white hunters are daring," said the eagle. "One even pointed his stick at me. If I had not flown quickly into the sky . . . I felt the rush of a hot ball through my tail feathers. I almost plummeted to the earth."

"*Hinh!*" wailed Iktomi. "These must be very foolish hunters to want to kill you. You are sacred to the Lakota."

The eagle preened. "They are not like the Lakota," Iktomi heard the disgust in her voice. "Have you seen a white man, Iktomi?"

"Yes. I have seen many of them. They are tearing into Mother Earth."

"They are not the only kind of *wasicu*," she said. "There are also those who drive the Lakota from their land and kill them if they dare to fight back."

Even as she spoke to Iktomi, the eagle was alert to all sounds and movement below. "Hush!" she ordered Iktomi and her eaglets. She turned her head from side to side, looking with one eye and then the other. "There—see the smoke rising?"

Iktomi shaded his eyes with a hand and peered into the lowering sun. At first he saw only rolling prairie, but then his eyes focused on plumes of smoke wafting upward. His ears heard sharp, repeated cracks that, had it been winter, might have been trees snapping in the cold. His nose quivered at the sharp wisps of smoke that floated up to the nest. The eaglets burrowed into the nest.

"What is it?" Iktomi quavered, suddenly as frightened as the eaglets.

"The firesticks," the eagle sadly explained, turning an eye to Iktomi. "Make yourself small, trickster," she ordered, "and climb upon my back. I will take you to see what the whites do."

Iktomi hesitated, but he was curious, and it would be a long walk to where the firesticks boomed and smoked. "You will not let me fall?" he asked as he willed himself smaller.

The eagle did not answer but turned to permit Iktomi to climb upon her back. He had barely grasped hold of her feathers when her wings lifted in strong, slow beats. Higher and higher she soared. The air streamed over her head and made Iktomi's eyes tear. He blinked them away, then the eagle cried, "Look!"

She spread her wings wide in a descending glide, and Iktomi gasped in horror. He saw blue-clad soldiers on horses, firing smoking sticks at the Lakota women and children running to the draws. The loud rifle cracks blended into a constant roar, and a pall of smoke from the guns mingled with that from burning teepees.

"Where are the warriors?" Iktomi cried.

The eagle glided lower and Iktomi saw the warriors sprawled lifeless. From the draws came the terrifying screams of women and children. They were soon silenced in the roar of rifle fire.

Iktomi heard a rough voice shout a command and the firing stopped. Now there was only silence. The eagle changed direction, and Iktomi clutched her feathers.

She soared up and again glided down. Iktomi's nostrils quivered as they caught the odor before his eyes saw the cause of the stench of decay. Bile rose in his throat; his stomach heaved.

Iktomi's eyes bulged. What they saw was more than his mind could believe. As far as Iktomi could see, the prairie was strewn with bloated, rotting buffalo carcasses.

"Eeeee!" Iktomi wailed. He buried his head in the eagle's neck as her wings carried them away from the dreadful carnage. "How can this be?" Iktomi sobbed. "The buffalo dead. The Lakota dead." His tears seeped into the eagle's feathers. Gently she carried Iktomi toward earth. Sadness and pity filled her heart. The trickster was related to the Lakota—he could not live without them.

"How can this be?" Iktomi mourned. "What will I do?

"No buffalo—no people—How will I eat?" Iktomi sobbed, absorbed in his selfish misery. He did not feel the eagle stiffening at his words. Abruptly she swooped to the side, and Iktomi fell.

"Farewell, Iktomi," his ears heard as his hands grasped the empty air. His sobs became terrified wails blending with the eagle's shrill screams.

"Foolish Iktomi. You will have to learn to live without the people."

TEN

The Settlers

Troll stood on the knoll where Iktomi had left him. From it he could survey the farm in the valley below. He came here every evening and watched until his humans went to bed. It was just like he had done in Norway, but of course he had no cave to shelter him, and here even after the summer sunset the night was hot.

Troll sighed, the vision of that far-off beautiful land vivid in his mind. He was glad to have found Thor, Oline, and Olaf, but how he missed his homeland! He gazed at the setting sun spreading gold and purple rays into the wide, cloudless sky. He wiped the sweat from his face; it was hot.

Thor's farm spread across gently rolling acres with the Big Sioux River winding through it. It was good land, Troll had often heard Thor declare. The man exulted in the ripening wheat in a field that was four times the size of the Svendsgaard in Norway. Troll, surveying the waving green and yellow grain, shared Thor's pride. Troll knew that Thor could never have plowed so large a field with only Olaf's help. Troll had made the labor easier.

He had been a silent, invisible partner to Thor's labors, first in plowing up the tough sod from which they built a shanty. Unseen, Troll had helped build the frame house that had replaced the sod shanty. He had loosened the tough sod so that Thor and Olaf could dig into the hillside for a shelter for the animals. This dugout made do as a barn until Thor could build the real thing.

Troll remembered the chore of cutting the tough prairie grass for hay for the cows' and horses' winter feed. He had accompanied Olaf to cut firewood, using his weight to fell the trees and spare the boy endless chopping. He had lessened Olaf's burden by helping to drag the trees to the farm where the boy cut stove-sized logs.

Thor, Oline, Olaf, and Troll worked from sunup to sundown with such intensity that there was little time for play. At first Troll expected his family to relax when his unseen aid helped them quickly finish their tasks. But Thor found more chores for Olaf, who was often so weary at supper that he barely managed to eat before collapsing in his bed. Troll pitied the boy but knew that Thor was fair with Olaf, giving him a portion of the harvest against the day when he would be of age to claim his own homestead.

Troll also helped care for Oline's garden, weeding and carrying water while the humans slept. Oline marveled at the richness of the soil and its perpetual moistness even when it didn't rain. "Why is this?" she asked Thor, who, weary from his labors, shrugged.

Olaf, only half joking, said, "Maybe there's a troll around the farm to help us."

"Don't be foolish!" Thor thundered angrily. "Trolls are myths of Norway and have no place in America!" The young farmer no longer believed in trolls, a fact that saddened and hurt Troll. But when Thor forbade Oline and Olaf to sing the old songs, Troll had been helplessly furious.

"This is a new world," Thor had said. "We don't need old songs to make you homesick. We must not think of Norway but only of America and being Americans!"

Troll fretted, but there was no way to change Thor's mind. Troll was sad because he was unable to keep part of his promise to Mette to help her children remember Norway. But he had faithfully fulfilled the rest of the vow; he had helped the little family prosper in their short time in America.

They had two cows that Olaf milked and cared for because, as Thor explained to the reluctant boy, Oline did not have time to do that. She was busy with her flock of chickens and geese; she cooked their meals, cleaned, sewed new clothes, and mended the old. Once a week she baked bread and did the laundry. These were chores Troll could not assist with, but he knew he eased her burden by caring for the garden.

The oxen had been replaced by a team of strong horses for the field work, and, when hitched to the wagon, the team carried the family into town for supplies, on social calls to neighbors, and to church.

After many other Norwegian immigrant families had settled in the area, they met for worship whenever a traveling pastor visited. One of them had donated land for the church, and all the men joined in the building. Troll had also helped build the church.

Troll had been excited when more Norwegians arrived, hoping that another troll or a nisse had come with the settlers. But none had, and the new human arrivals were just as determined as Thor to forget Norwegian ways and become Americans. Some had already changed the spelling of their names to more American-sounding versions. Thor was thinking of changing Svendson to Swenson.

Still, Troll reflected, he was happy to be with his humans — not content as he had been in Norway but satisfied that he was fulfilling part of his promise to that faraway mother.

With the coming of more settlers, after the church a school was built, and Thor made Olaf attend. Troll thought it was generous of Thor to spare the boy from constant farm work. But each evening of a school day, Thor made Olaf repeat the day's English lesson so that he and Oline could also learn. Then Thor insisted that the family speak only English — no more Norwegian.

Sorrowfully, Troll recalled how Oline persisted in trying to keep Norwegian customs in her home. On their first Christmas, the young woman had wept because there were no evergreens, but she decorated the house with bits of ribbon. Neither was there flour nor sugar for the traditional cream cake or *fatigmand*. Instead, Oline made cornbread and served it with molasses. Olaf had gone hunting, hoping to bring home a deer, but he enjoyed the rabbit stew Oline had cheerfully prepared. Before sitting down to the meal, Oline had urged Thor to join hands with her and Olaf while they sang Norwegian carols. Thor did not forbid them to do so but refused to join in, saying, "This should not be done in America."

Oline tried to make Christmas as joyful as she could, especially for Olaf, who she knew missed his parents. But then, so did she. There was no milk to make porridge, so Oline placed a slice of cornbread outside the door. There was no wheat to tie in a sheaf to put out for the birds, so Oline sprinkled kernels of corn on the bare, frozen ground.

"Ah, it was a sad time." Troll remembered how he had wept with Oline while she strewed the corn, his heart sad at her distress.

That first winter was long and cold with a perpetual wind that chilled Troll to his ancient bones.

"Wind!" Troll said as if the word were a curse. He hated it more than anything else in this new land. He had shivered and suffered through the winter huddled against the lee side of the cabin, for he was too large to take shelter with the animals in the dugout. How he had longed for the snug comfort of his cave!

Now, on this hot evening, he welcomed the breeze that evaporated the sweat from his huge body, cooling him after the heat of the day. "Ahhh," he sighed. The summer heat of the prairies was as extreme in its discomfort as was the winter cold.

Troll lowered his weary body to the tough grass and rested his head in his hands. How he longed for Norway—the forests, his mountain, his cave, and another being to talk with.

"Oh, Mother," he moaned, "I never should have listened to your pleas to come to this terrible land. I am so alone!" A groaning sob shuddered through him. He lifted his head to look at the evening star and wept.

"I hear him!" Oline peered out into the gathering dusk. Troll looked down at the house.

"I did hear him!" Oline cried again, stepping out into the yard. "Let me go!" Oline pulled away from Thor, who clutched her arm.

"It's only the wind, Oline," Thor said gently. "Come to bed."

Oline jerked free and gazed frantically about her. "I heard a troll—I know I did—just like the mountain troll at home."

"There are no trolls," Thor said patiently. "Not here, nor in Norway. They are myths created for children."

"Thor," Oline cried. "You have become—so unfeeling. You've become like this land—hard and cruel!"

"Stop it!" Thor commanded. "You heard the wind! Calm yourself before you harm the babe with your fanciful thoughts!"

"Babe?" Troll wondered, and then he understood. Oline was going to have a baby. He laughed with joy and clapped his hands.

"There! Hear him?" Oline clutched Thor's arm. "Did you hear?"

Thor shook his head and Oline angrily pounded her fist on his arm. "I heard him!" she raged. "Just as my mother and your mother heard him at home!"

70

Thor held the struggling woman tightly to him. "Oline," he begged, and Troll heard the pain in the man's voice. "Please, please stop." Oline collapsed, clinging to Thor, who stroked her hair. "Oline, don't cry. It is because of the baby that you are so upset. Shh, shh, don't cry."

Troll's heart pounded wildly as he watched Thor lead Oline to the house. "I AM here!" he shouted.

Oline lifted her head and looked up at the knoll where Troll stood. "See," he cried to the woman, who seemed to look at him, "I AM here!"

"Did you hear, Thor?" Oline pointed at the knoll. "Olaf," she cried to the boy, who had come out of the house. "Did you hear, Olaf?"

The boy stared at he knoll. "I—I'm not sure," he stammered.

Oline moved out of Thor's arms and took Olaf's hand. "Your mother often spoke of hearing the troll and even seeing him. Remember?"

Olaf nodded but dared not speak. He jerked away from Oline as Thor's harsh voice thundered, "Olaf! I forbid you to encourage Oline's fancies!"

Troll held his breath as Olaf stared at his angry brother. The boy was as tall as the man, his shoulders almost as broad. He lifted his chin said, "Mother used to tell me about our troll."

Thor's face flushed, and he took a step toward the boy. Troll feared that he would strike Olaf. But Thor stopped and took a deep breath. "Of course she did," he spoke patiently, as if to a small child. "Mothers all over Norway tell their children stories of trolls and nisse—and don't forget about the hulder. But," Thor's voice was firm, "they are only stories!" He glared at Olaf, who backed away.

Oline also moved away from her angry husband, but when he held out his hand she placed hers in it. "Let us go to bed," Thor said, and he led her into the house.

Troll sank sadly to the ground. "Oline heard me," he whispered. "I know she did!" He gazed down at the lighted window of the house. "She is almost a mother; perhaps that is why she heard me." Troll brightened at the thought. "Mothers and children can hear and see trolls."

Hope stirred in the giant's heart. "When the child is born, Oline will also be able to see me if I wish. And," he smiled happily, "Oline will speak to me."

Troll stretched out on the hard earth. "When the baby comes—" He smiled up at the stars.

ELEVEN

Leave Us, Iktomi

Iktomi groaned as he awakened. "Ow," complained his legs, arms, head — every part of his body. Then he remembered. "*Wambli —* she dropped me!"

Iktomi's eyes looked up at the star. "Why, it is night!" He was amazed, for it had been daylight when he had flown on the eagle's back.

Iktomi willed his body to roll over. He saw stars below him, "Whaa — ? Am I upside down or has the sky fallen?" He closed his eyes and his mind cleared. The stars were reflected in the slow-moving river. Stiffly he crawled to the water and drank until his stomach gurgled, "Enough." Wearily Iktomi lay back and addressed the stars.

"What will I do?" he moaned. "The people are gone." Self-pitying tears seeped from his eyes, but then his self-pity turned to a flow of grief as he remembered the dead and dying people.

Iktomi sat up and yanked at his hair. "*Aaii!*" he wailed. "I will

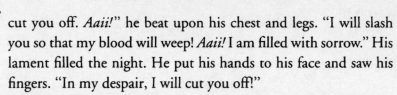

cut you off. *Aaii!*" he beat upon his chest and legs. "I will slash
you so that my blood will weep! *Aaii!* I am filled with sorrow." His
lament filled the night. He put his hands to his face and saw his
fingers. "In my despair, I will cut you off!"

"How can you?" the voice in his head interrupted his wails.
"You have no knife."

"True," Iktomi agreed, and his hands swiped at his tears. "I'll
find a knife tomorrow," he promised. He lay on the sand and
slept.

The sun was high in the sky when Iktomi again awakened. The
day was already hot, and Iktomi heard only the call of his dry
throat and empty stomach.

He walked along the river, his mind thinking of ways to catch
a fish without making a spear. He spotted a turtle slowly crawling
along the muddy bank. Quickly Iktomi grabbed it.

"Hah!" he triumphed. "Turtle will make a good meal!"

But the turtle pulled itself tightly into its shell. Iktomi pounded
and shook, but the turtle was safe. Iktomi peered into the shell
and saw bright eyes glaring at him.

"Come out, little brother," Iktomi crooned.

"No," the turtle whispered. "I am afraid to come out."

"Do not be frightened, little brother," Iktomi soothed. His
mind was busily thinking of ways to kill the turtle and get the
meat out of the shell.

"No," answered the turtle. "I know you, Iktomi. You will do
some terrible thing to me. Perhaps you'll throw me in the water
so that I will drown. Then you will eat me."

"What?" Iktomi said. "Throw you in the river?"

"Oh, no," said the frightened turtle. "Please, Iktomi. If you are going to kill me, please be merciful. Don't throw me in the water!"

Iktomi was ecstatic—the stupid turtle had told him how to kill it. "Oh, ho, little brother," he cried, and he lifted his arms and threw the turtle into the river.

"Nooo!" the turtle wailed as it sailed through the air. It landed with a splash and sank.

Iktomi waded into the river, his eyes watchful and his hands ready to grab the dead turtle when it floated to the surface.

"Ha, ha, ha!" Iktomi heard gurgling laughter from downstream. He looked and saw the turtle swimming safely away.

"You tricked me!" Iktomi screamed and splashed after the turtle. His feet sank in the mud and water filled his mouth. He floundered, coughed, flapped his arms, and kicked against the strong current hidden beneath the sluggish surface. Now he was in the deep channel and whirling downstream. He forgot the turtle and struggled to swim out of the current's grasp. A log crashed into his shoulder, and he pushed it away as it battered him into a whirlpool.

"Grab the log!" the voice inside his head ordered, and his hands obeyed. "Kick!" the voice screamed, and Iktomi's legs moved and splashed out of the whirlpool.

At last Iktomi's feet touched bottom as the log carried him to shore. Exhausted, Iktomi fell on the sand, coughing water from his mouth and blowing it from his nose. His heart stilled its frantic beats, and Iktomi sat up.

There were three ragged teepees in the trees along the shore. "Lakota!" Iktomi jumped to his feet. "I have found the people!"

A woman came out of a teepee and turned a broiling fish over the fire. She looked up and saw Iktomi running toward her, but she made no move to welcome him.

"*Hau,* sister," Iktomi greeted. "Happy my heart is to see you. I have been searching and searching for the Lakota." Iktomi babbled on in his joy, but his eyes were on the fish.

The woman stood upright. "Go away," she said in a weary voice. "I have nothing to feed you."

"Oh, sister," Iktomi wailed. "I have had such terrible times— I cannot tell you how bad. I will only take one small bite of the fish."

"Bad times?" the woman gave a bitter laugh. "You do not know about bad times! Have you seen your child blown apart by a firestick? Does your beloved lie dying from the firestick's wound?"

She stepped closer and grabbed Iktomi's arm. "Where are your wounds? All of our warriors are wounded—or dead. Did you fight to save us?" The angry glitter faded from her eyes, leaving them dull and hopeless. She dropped Iktomi's arm.

"Oh, sister," Iktomi pleaded for understanding. "You know I have no weapons. How could I fight? Indeed, I had no people to defend—I have been so alone," he wailed.

Other women and men emerged from the ragged lodges and Iktomi's heart was stricken at their appearance. Thin and gaunt, eyes dulled with despair, none smiled to see the trickster. For even though the Lakota knew of Iktomi's wily ways, they had loved him. He had been proud when they told their children of his exploits, even though they laughed and cautioned the young ones not to act like the trickster.

Iktomi had believed that he was a necessary part of Lakota life. But these poor people did not welcome Iktomi.

"Go, Iktomi!" The weak order came from the one uninjured warrior of the remnant band.

"You can't send me away," Iktomi blustered. "I too am Lakota! You need me." Then he begged, "I need you."

"Leave us, Iktomi. We have nothing for you," the warrior said sadly. "We no longer need you."

Iktomi's heart was pierced by the cruel words. His eyes spilled tears. Woefully, he stared at the pitiful people and they at him.

"What will you do?" he asked, finally understanding their despair.

"We will go to the reservation," was the quiet reply.

Iktomi was horrified. "But you will die there!"

"We are already dead," the warrior said, and the people turned their backs on Iktomi.

TWELVE

Necessary Companions

"Am I going mad?" Troll wondered.

He thought of all the trolls he had known or had heard of, but he could not remember one who had gone insane. In Norway, he recalled, there were mean, nasty, cruel trolls and mischievous, fun-loving, happy trolls. Tiny trolls, giant trolls, trolls with one eye, and even a troll with two heads.

There were trolls who didn't need the company of other trolls — especially the company of female trolls, which was a good thing because there were few of them.

Troll nodded and mumbled to himself. "Most of us are sturdy, stolid—We don't anger easily but have fearful tempers when roused."

He stopped walking, concentrating to remember the trolls in Norway's long history. "Yah," he nodded, "there was a Viking troll. Oh, and there was the one who lived underground because he couldn't stand sunlight. Many, many trolls—all kinds—but none could exist without humans.

"But I must be the first to go mad," Troll declared to the wind. "For when I speak and when I shout—no matter how loudly—I cannot hear myself! I surely am mad!"

Troll shook his shaggy head and nodded aimlessly forward as he had done ever since he had left his humans' homestead.

Mournfully, his huge body aching with grief, Troll had fled because Oline's baby was dead. And with the infant's death, Troll's life with his humans was over. Oline would never hear or see him because she could not tell her child about trolls. Thor denied the existence of trolls, and Olaf—Troll's grief surged into despair as he thought of the boy.

Olaf had fled the house as Oline labored to give birth. He sat on the knoll overlooking the house, watching and waiting with the unseen Troll beside him. Troll sensed Olaf's loneliness and listened in mute sympathy as the boy spoke. "I wish Mother— Father—," Olaf's voice broke into bitter sobs.

Gently, Troll's hand touched Olaf's hair. "Olaf, Olaf," Troll murmured.

The boy tensed as if he had heard Troll and felt the kindly touch. "If only Troll were really here," he sighed.

"I am!" Troll cried, and he willed himself visible.

But Olaf clamped his hands over his ears and squeezed his eyes shut. "No! Thor is right! Thinking of home—Mother, Father, of trolls—only makes me sad. No more!" Olaf jumped to his feet and ran down the hill.

Troll sighed and sat down to wait for the baby's birth. But when the infant came it did not draw a single breath, and Troll left his humans.

Bitterly the giant had wandered the prairies, his grief turning to anger. Loudly he shouted, cursing the mother who had sent him to this cruel and barren land.

"Why did I listen to your false pleas?" he cried into the wind. "Oh, woman, you lied! You said I could return to Norway if I did not like America—You knew that I would never see Norway again!" Troll raged on until suddenly he realized that he was shouting and his lips were moving, but he could not hear himself. That's when he'd decided that he must have been driven to madness by this country.

He walked the plains as he had when he had lost his humans, but now he did not care. He ignored the scratches and bruises on his feet and the constant, cold wind that chilled and burned his skin. He waded many streams and did not stop to drink. Day and night he walked, lurching and staggering, stumbling and falling; he forced himself to go on. For the first time in his life, the ageless troll wished for death.

He floundered and splashed across a muddy river and didn't feel the water freezing his beard and stiffening his ragged clothes. Snow engulfed him as he struggled to climb steep bluffs. When at last he reached the top, harsh winds bent him double against a stinging blizzard. Still he went on.

Å kjøre vatten, å kjøre ve', he tried to sing through the rime on his lips, the melody whirling through his mindless pain. Darkness surrounded him, but still he stumbled on, not caring or feeling the deadly cold. Then he fell.

Down he rolled and slid, over and through deep drifts until he tumbled blindly into a tree. This time he did not try to rise.

Å kjøre vatten— His chapped lips barely formed the words. "Ah," Troll signed, "why do I sing? I can't hear myself—so I am not singing. No one hears." Wearily he rested his head against the trunk of the tree and closed his eyes.

"I hear," a familiar voice grumbled.

Troll's eyes opened. "What?" he asked, afraid to believe what he had heard.

"I said, I hear you!" the unseen voice grumbled on. "Who could not hear you—crashing into trees and singing that stupid song!"

Troll jerked upright, staring into the swirling snow, and cracked his head on a low branch.

"Watch out! You clumsy giant! You'll knock me down!"

"Iktomi?" Troll asked in amazed disbelief. "Is it you?" Then he roared with delight, for he could hear himself.

"Aaahh! Ooooh! Haaaa!" Troll yelled and laughed. "I speak! I hear!" He grabbed the low branch and pulled himself to his feet.

"Stop!" yelled Iktomi. "Don't shake the tree—I'll fall!"

Troll reached toward the voice and found the trickster clinging to a branch. Laughing with joy, Troll plucked Iktomi into his arms. Holding him tightly, he danced about the tree, crashing through branches and snow. Laughing and weeping, "Iktomi! My friend! How happy I am to find you!"

At last Troll stopped. He was overwhelmed with joy but was so tired. He put the struggling Iktomi down.

"You—you," Iktomi sputtered and then smiled up at Troll's wide grin. "And I am happy to find you."

Quietly, the two shook hands, unheeding of the howling wind and stinging snow. But Troll began to shiver. His legs trembling, he sank weakly to the earth. "So c—c—c—cold," he stuttered through chattering teeth.

"Yes," agreed Iktomi. "Where's my blanket? I can't lose it." He waded through the snow around the tree and found the blanket.

"I did not know what beast was crashing down the hill," Iktomi explained as he shook snow from the blanket. "I climbed the tree to get out of its way." He wrapped the blanket about himself. "I have been traveling for many days, trying to decide where I should stay for the winter," Iktomi chatted on, pleased to have someone to talk to. "I traveled west, hoping to find more Lakota. I did not find them, but I did find a shack, like whites build on the land.

"I was wary that a *wasicu* would ambush me with a firestick, but the shack was empty. I stayed there for two sleeps—that's where I found the blanket and *this,*" he proudly pulled a knife from his waist.

"Where have you come from?" he asked Troll. "Why didn't you stay with your humans?"

Troll did not answer. Iktomi moved to where the giant lay under the tree. He peered at the huge form already covered with snow. He prodded with his foot. "Troll?" Iktomi called. When the giant did not respond, he yelled "Troll!" He reached down, grabbed Troll's hair, and shook him. But the giant did not answer.

"You stupid giant!" Iktomi frantically shook Troll. "Wake up! Move! Don't sleep! You won't wake up! TROLL!" He banged the giant's head against the tree.

"Ehh?" Troll muttered. He opened one eye. "Leave me alone — so tired," he whispered. "Let me sleep."

Iktomi, dreadfully frightened at Troll's sluggish response, pulled and tugged at the giant's arm. "Move! Get up! You must not sleep! You will freeze to death!"

Listlessly, Troll sat and tried to wave Iktomi aside, but the trickster persisted. "Up! Come, we must find shelter!" he ordered, and shoved the giant to his feet. "Good! Now walk! There is a cave — near —" Iktomi grunted and pulled, leading the lethargic Troll through the blinding blizzard.

The pair struggled up a steep slope. "Keep going," Iktomi panted. He pushed and kicked at Troll. "There's the cave!" He braced his back against Troll's legs and shoved. The giant fell into the cave.

Breathing heavily, Iktomi rubbed Troll's face, hands, and feet, all the while grumbling and pleading, "Ugly, stupid one. Wake up!" until Troll was alert. Then Iktomi leaned against the wall, wiping perspiration from his head. "What a nuisance you are," he said, but he moved closer to Troll and covered them both as best he could with his blanket.

THIRTEEN

Paha Sapa

Iktomi and Troll awakened at the same time. They lay close together. Troll's feet and part of his legs were covered by the thin blanket under which Iktomi huddled. They were cold but alive after two days in the shallow cave with the wind howling at its mouth.

Now there was a stillness, and they listened, wondering what it was they did or did not hear. "The wind," Iktomi said, and he threw off the blanket. "The wind has died. The storm is over."

Iktomi crawled to the opening of the cave and punched at the snow that had drifted it almost shut. Troll pushed with his hands and the sunlight streamed in. The two blinked and peered out.

"Where's the snow?" Troll wondered. Except for sheltered areas around bushes, trees, and the cave, the grayish tan prairie was empty of snow and life. Troll had expected to see the land covered with white as it would have been in Norway after a winter storm. "Is this all?" he asked, kicking at the drift about the cave.

Iktomi nodded. He waved his hand before him. "This is the western prairie. The north wind sweeps the snow before it."

Iktomi turned back to the cave, picked up his blanket, and headed down to the prairie. "Let us go," he said to Troll.

"Where?" Troll asked, but he followed. Never again did he want to be alone on the plains.

"To Paha Sapa."

"Black Hills?" Troll asked. "The mountains of the Lakota?" His heart beat faster at the thought of seeing mountains again.

Iktomi led Troll across windswept prairies devoid of life—no people, no buffalo or other game. The land rolled on and the pair walked. Iktomi ignored his complaining stomach, but his eyes moved restlessly in search of food.

Night came and the travelers stopped along a frozen stream. Troll used a tree branch to punch a hole in the ice so they could drink. Iktomi peeled and sharpened a straight twig, gathered dry grass, and set a flat piece of bark within it. He took the sharp stick, set its point on the bark, and twirled it between his hands.

"What are you doing?" Troll asked, but Iktomi didn't hear because he was so intent on his task. Troll bent over and watched, and then he saw a wisp of smoke. Without being asked he turned and began gathering dry twigs and snapping large branches for a campfire.

"HO!" Iktomi shouted, and he fed the flickering flame with dry grass followed by the twigs Troll gave him. Soon the two were basking by the fire. Although warm, Iktomi could not ignore the growls from his empty stomach, so he rose. "I will look for some cherries that may still be on — Oh, here are some rose hips."

"Let me use your knife," Troll said. "I will fashion a spear from this branch and try to catch some fish." He lay down, most of his body over the ground and his head over the hole in the ice. Patiently he waited, then he quickly jabbed and pulled out a fish.

So the two had a sparse meal, but they were content.

The next day they walked on. The land imperceptibly rose, first into rolling hills and then higher until Iktomi stopped and pointed, and Troll saw the Black Hills.

The hills were not truly black — more a smudgy gray against the horizon — and they were not the mountains Troll yearned to see. He had been looking for snow-capped peaks. But he said nothing. They strode on, the climb steepening. Then, much to Troll's delight, snow-covered peaks rose above the dark, blue-green spruce and pines that seemed almost black from the plains.

They moved into a forest, and Troll laughed and joyfully gazed at the trees — pines, taller than he, and aspen bordering meadows. And there was snow — deep snow piled in cones on the arms of trees. And there was no wind!

They saw deer, elk, and rabbits and heard birds in the trees. Iktomi told Troll that there were also bears that they would not see until spring.

Troll wanted to surge ahead through the snow up to the rocky precipices he saw above the trees, but Iktomi moved slowly, huffing and panting for breath in the thin air as he struggled through deep snow. Impatiently, Troll plodded behind the smaller being until Iktomi again paused to catch his breath and rest. "Let me carry you," Troll suggested.

Iktomi looked up in surprise. Why had he not thought of riding on Troll's shoulders? Then he realized his mind's voice had not been scheming or plotting since he had left the Lakota at the river. He thought of that time, and his heart ached for the people but not for himself. Now, as he heard Troll ask again if he wanted to ride on his shoulders, Iktomi felt a pleasurable pride in his being able to take care of himself without the people. And he, all by himself, had cared for Troll, keeping the giant alive.

"They said they did not need me," Iktomi thought aloud. "Neither do I need them."

"What?" Troll asked, and Iktomi laughed.

"Yes, my friend, carry me, and we will make better time."

Perched atop Troll's shoulders, Iktomi guided the giant through the mountains. As they traveled, Iktomi told Troll of the Lakotas' rejection and the pain it had caused him. Troll had already told of why he had left his humans to wander blindly, thinking he was mad, in the plains.

"Humans are unreliable," Troll concluded, and Iktomi agreed.

As different as the plodding, melancholy giant was from the smaller, adventurous trickster, both understood that if they stayed together they would survive.

Iktomi guided Troll to a spacious cave deep within the needle spires of the Black Hills, and there the two ageless beings made their home.

They were satisfied, if not content, in their exile. Time had no relevance for them and the years passed. Alone, save for the animals and birds, they led a life of stultifying sameness: day after day, they rose with the sun and slept with its setting. In between, their activities varied with the seasons.

Troll rarely ventured farther than the stream below no matter the time of year. His heavy steps trod a deep path from the cave to the creek where he bathed and fished and along whose banks he gathered berries. In the winter he rarely had to chip a hole in the ice because the rapidly moving stream seldom froze solid.

Except for the snowy months, Troll spent most of his time on the boulder he had moved to the right of the cave's entrance — just as his rock in Norway had been placed. He had worn a comfortable seat on it as he sunned himself, contemplating the Black Hills.

"They are not truly mountains," he complained to Iktomi, who soon wearied of Troll's comparing the sacred Paha Sapa to Norway's peaks.

Only in the winter did Troll think the Black Hills were like his homeland. Then the snow fell, rarely disturbed by the wind, until the cave's entrance was buried and Troll had to clear a tunnel, just as he had in Norway. Then Troll longed for human contact. Winter after winter he told Iktomi of the generations of Norwegian mothers who had left him food and warm, homespun blankets. Now he had only pine boughs for a bed with a cover of plaited strips of aspen bark.

It was in the winters that Troll's melancholia deepened to dismal depths, and he sang song after song while tears streamed down his face to puddle on the floor of the cave.

Had there been humans to hear, they would have been mystified by the desolate, mournful strains filling the still winter silence. They would puzzle over the counterpoint drum beats and chanting that accompanied the dirgelike airs. For Iktomi sang too.

At first, he sang in self-defense against Troll's endless wailings. But the Lakota battle songs, death songs, and love songs relieved his restless frustration at being confined to the cave.

Winter after winter, the two sang—day after day until spring released them. Then Iktomi fled the cave and Troll.

Restless and curious, Iktomi wandered the Black Hills and came to know every rock, stream, and tree. He learned the habits of the animals and became a skillful hunter and trapper. He clumsily fashioned a bow, cursing himself for not watching Lakota bow makers more carefully. Troll made the arrows and arrowheads, as he was more patient in the task of chipping stones to smoothly sharpened points and fitting them to the shafts. Then Iktomi fastened the feathers to make the arrow soar; Troll's fingers were too big.

Iktomi snared rabbits, ermine, mink, and sometimes beaver. He and Troll skinned the animals and ruined many hides before they learned to tan them and fashion footwear. The small animals also fed them, for Troll refused to help Iktomi hunt the deer or elk that ranged undisturbed through the pines below the cave.

Troll and Iktomi bickered and argued about hunting and about how to make arrows and snares. They disagreed on shapes of moccasins and how to weave aspen bark into blankets. Then one or the other or both would sulk, and days would pass without a single word passing between them until they forgot what had caused the tiff.

Day after day, season after season, the years passed, and then humans came to the Black Hills.

FOURTEEN

Alone No Longer

Iktomi found them first. His ears caught the sound of men's voices. At first he tried to ignore the unfamiliar sound, but his curiosity made him wonder, "Who is it?"

Warily, Iktomi crawled to the lip of a rock and cautiously looked down. "*Wasicus!*" he whispered sharply and ducked as one of the men looked up and waved toward the rocks about him. "What are they doing?"

These were not farmers who plowed the land, but they, too, tore into Mother Earth. Using sharp iron picks on long wooden handles, the men pounded away at the rocks and shale of the mountains. Loud clangs rang through the forest, startling birds into flight, and the deer and elk fled.

Iktomi crept away after he saw a firestick leaning against a tree near where a white miner was digging. He stayed on the higher peaks and watched. He saw other white men intently staring into pans in which they swirled water and gravel. He found *wasicus* directing strangers who wore loose-fitting garments and had a single long braid hanging down their backs. Their skin color was not white, but it was not bronze like the Lakotas. When their white boss yelled, the smaller men dug faster.

Iktomi did not like all the noise that the men were making and returned to cave. He reported what he had seen to Troll.

"Humans?" Troll was excited yet frightened. "Did you see any Norwegians?"

"How would I know?" Iktomi shrugged. "All *wasicus* look alike. But there was a new kind of human—one not white nor like my people. They have one long braid and their eyes slant. I don't know who they are."

"What should we do?" Troll asked.

Again Iktomi shrugged. "What can we do? Let's ignore them and maybe they'll go away."

But the humans stayed, and more of them came to burrow into the sacred hills. Iktomi couldn't stay away from their activity. He watched them dig into a huge boulder and lay a box at its base. Then all the men ran and hid behind trees or other rocks. There was a brief moment of quiet, then Iktomi recoiled in horror as the boulder lifted in a cloud of smoke and dust. A boom, louder than any thunder, and an unseen force threw him on his back.

Later he awoke, his ears ringing and his body aching from landing on sharp stones. He jumped to his feet and ran to the cave. "Troll, the *wasicus* are causing thunder to blast away boulders."

Troll looked up from his seat by the cave. "Dynamite," he said.

"What?" Iktomi yelled.

"Dynamite," Troll repeated. "I remember such blasts were used in Norway."

"I can't hear you," Iktomi rubbed his ears. "All I hear is noise in my head."

Iktomi had been deafened by the loud blast. Days passed and he moaned and groaned around the cave. Finally he could hear again, and he returned to watch the white men.

Where the boulder had been, iron tracks were being pounded into the earth. He heard a moaning kind of a whistle and saw an iron monster chugging and belching smoke as it labored up the steep tracks. That evening when he told Troll the giant said, "It's an engine that pulls the cars like I rode in with my humans so long ago."

One morning Troll was making his habitual trek to the stream to bathe and perhaps fish when the sound of human voices froze him in the path. He heard the bass voices of men speaking and the lilt of female laughter. Troll turned and lumbered quietly back to the cave.

"What is it?" Iktomi noticed the giant's agitation.

"Humans," Troll motioned to the stream below.

Iktomi clambered through the spires and peered down. Yes, there they were, two men climbing through the rocks. He looked at Troll and Troll stared back, then in silent agreement they moved to repel the humans.

Troll roared, and his voice, thundering through the tall needle spires, seemed to come from all directions. He pried a boulder off his hidden precipice and bounced it down the hill. It clattered and scattered smaller rocks into a small slide that rumbled toward the men.

Iktomi scampered through the pines where two horses were tethered to trees. He stopped in alarm as he saw a woman standing by a third horse. She saw him and screamed for the men, who were running from Troll's rockslide.

Iktomi retreated up the hill. Hidden among the pines he circled the woman, who had mounted and was frantically trying to calm her rearing horse. Iktomi gathered pine cones and pelted the horse. It snorted and bolted down the mountain with the woman clinging to the saddle horn.

Gleefully, Iktomi ran to the other horses, lifted the packs strapped to their backs, and slipped their tethers. "Haw!" he shouted, and he slapped one horse's rump. It turned and charged down the mountain, the other close behind.

Stifling his laughter, Iktomi dodged behind trees as the two men raced after the horses. Thunder seemed to boom as Troll roared again. Iktomi aimed pine cones and hooted with joy as they struck the head and shoulders of the retreating men.

The echo of Troll's roar faded, the crashing slide stilled, and once again it was quiet in the Black Hills.

But it didn't last. More and more curious humans came, and Iktomi and Troll drove them away. They came to enjoy these encounters, which supplied days of conversation. They never hurt the humans but laughed in delight to see their undignified, hasty retreat.

Now, Iktomi and Troll lived more comfortably in the cave with supplies taken from the humans. Cooking pots, coffee, sugar, cornmeal, bacon, and sometimes candy became a part of their life. They had rough wool blankets to warm them in the winters. They also had odd things such as a whistle on a string, a compass, and a map. Matches made fire-starting easier, and a pipe with tobacco delighted Iktomi.

Now their lives had excitement and purpose. Troll and Iktomi thrived on their defensive contact with humans, and by listening to the humans talk, they knew what was going on around them.

Iktomi still rambled through the hills while watching human activity from above. Besides the train, he saw horse-drawn wagons and stagecoaches, which in time gave way to noisy motor cars that filled the air with their foul smoke.

At first, Iktomi only watched from a distance, but after years of successfully repelling visitors near the cave, he had lost his fear of them. Nor could he stifle his curious mind, and he moved among the humans.

He strolled along the busy streets of a town he found that had sprung up in a gulch full of dead wood. Most of the white people ignored him or drew away—not in fear, but in disgust. Others teased and laughed at him.

"Hey, Injun, do a war dance," some urged.

"Don't scalp us!" jokesters cried, hands to their bushy heads, cringing in mock fear.

Still others were cruel. "I said dance, Injun," one ordered, and when Iktomi didn't, he pulled short firesticks from his belt and shot around the trickster's feet, making Iktomi hop and jump and cry out in terror.

A few white people were kind. Iktomi soon became a regular visitor to them because they gave him food.

"You must dress more respectably," one kind woman said, holding out trousers and a shirt. "But before you put them on you must bathe, and we'll cut your hair."

Iktomi fled. "I bathe in the stream. Never will a Lakota cut his hair!" he muttered as he ran.

Iktomi found some Lakotas in the Black Hills. There were six men with their women and many children. How happy Iktomi was to see them! "Oh, you have lived!" he happily called, but they ignored him. Then his joy turned to disgust as he watched. The men wore fake headdresses, mounted painted horses, and yelled as they made a mock attack on a stagecoach. Firesticks poked out of the coach, they popped and smoked, and the sham warriors fell from their horses and feigned death. The white audience cheered.

Later, the men danced wildly, stomping to the drumbeat while their shawled women quietly moved up and down on their heels in a circle around the men. Again the whites clapped and cheered and threw coins into the circle. To Iktomi's dismay, the men and the women pushed and shoved each other to get the money.

"Shame!" he cried. Iktomi was embarrassed for these people who seemed to have none of the dignity and pride of the Lakota.

He moved to stand by the children who were huddled by the canvas teepees outside the dance circle.

"*Hau*," he greeted. The children shrank from him, and one of the women ran to them.

"Who are you?" she called and gathered her children close.

"I am Iktomi," he smiled.

"Who?" asked one of the men as he came from the dance.

"Iktomi, the trickster of the Lakota," Iktomi proudly declared.

"Hah, hah," they laughed. "There's no such thing as an Iktomi." They turned back to dance.

Hurt and bewildered, Iktomi returned to the cave and sadly told Troll about the Lakota he had met. Troll was sympathetic. "I know, Iktomi," he said. "Humans don't believe in us anymore."

Troll was glad to have Iktomi back at the cave. He would never tell the trickster that he was missed when he went on one of his long treks, but Troll did not like being alone. So when Iktomi returned, he avidly listened to all that Iktomi told of seeing.

"Did you find any Norwegians?" Troll always asked, but Iktomi always said "No."

Then one day Iktomi came eagerly running up to the cave. "I found a nisse!" he called.

Troll was stunned. Even though he asked about Norwegians whenever Iktomi returned, he never expected to hear of them, let alone a nisse.

"Come," Iktomi said. "I will take you to him."

Troll rose. He hesitated. If a nisse was in this country, so were more Norwegians. What if they didn't know about trolls the way Iktomi's Lakota had not known of the trickster? His heart could not stand to be rejected again.

"Come," Iktomi called impatiently.

Slowly, Troll followed. Iktomi led him out of the mountains into the rolling foothills that flowed into the prairie. Troll's anxiety grew as they moved through lush grass and he stopped, startled by a sound he hadn't heard since he had left his humans. He looked down at the valley below.

"Moo, mooo, moo," cattle bawled as they were herded to higher pasture.

Troll gaped, "Where did all of these cattle come from?"

"Oh," Iktomi growled, "they're all over now. There's almost as many as there are *wasicus!* Come on, the place is over there." The trickster pointed and Troll saw a house and a barn. "A farm," he breathed.

"A ranch," Iktomi corrected. "The man who lives here calls it a ranch. The nisse is in the barn."

Troll stood before the barn, his heart pounding. "Ni—ni—," he started, but the sound caught in his throat. He cleared it, but before he could try again he heard "*Velkommen,*" and there was a nisse.

Troll stared at the small figure perched on the edge of the barn's roof.

"So," the nisse said, "the *Indianer* told the truth; there is a troll in this land. How did you get here?"

Troll told the nisse of his journey to America: the train ride, losing and finding his humans, and finally leaving them because they no longer believed he existed.

The nisse listened and then related how he had traveled with his humans on a trek much like the one Troll had made. "There were many of us nisse coming to America. So many of the humans were leaving Norway that we nisse had to go with them.

"We take care of their cattle and ensure a good harvest just as we did in Norway," explained the nisse. "That is, if our humans take care of us."

The troll and the nisse did not hear Iktomi say, "I'm leaving." They were too engrossed in speaking Norwegian and telling of their travails in America.

Irked at being ignored, the trickster waved and wandered through the foothills. Soon he found himself on the plains. "Alone," his mind's voice startled Iktomi. "I shouldn't have taken Troll to the nisse—now he has a friend." Bitter jealousy filled his heart, and the long-denied yearning for his own people made it ache. "Find them," his mind urged, and Iktomi looked over the prairie. "Find the Lakota."

But Iktomi remembered the ragged band along the river. "Leave us, Iktomi," they had said. He would never forget those cruel words, and he did not want to be unwanted ever again.

He knew that there were other Lakota who had survived, but if they were like the fools he had seen in Deadwood, they wouldn't know the trickster. "Go back to the cave," his heart cautioned. "There you are safe."

"It will always be there," his mind soothed. "Paha Sapa will always be a haven if you need one."

"I'm hungry," his stomach rumbled. Iktomi heeded its complaint and strode east through the tall grass.

His eyes roamed and searched as he walked. "No buffalo," he muttered, and then he spat in disgust as he saw another herd of cattle feeding where *tatanka* once grew fat.

He spotted a ridge of pines and headed toward it. From there he could scan the prairies for the Lakota. But he found the people before he climbed the ridge.

He ducked down and peered through the grass, studying the amazing scene. These people were not the dispirited band who had rejected him, nor were they the foolish ones who fought fake battles for the whites.

There were no teepees, but houses. The men and women wore clothing like the whites, and he heard them speak English.

"Careful," the voice in his head cautioned, "these people seem like *wasicus*—they may aim a firestick at us."

"But perhaps they'll give us meat," his stomach urged.

Iktomi stealthily moved among the houses. He peered into windows and listened at doors. Then he heard the children.

Two boys and two girls, one of them carrying a baby, came chattering and laughing into the yard. Iktomi, hiding behind a shed, watched them, delighting in their gaiety. It had been so long since he had heard a Lakota child laugh. They disappeared into the house. Carefully he crept to the window and peeked in at the children.

The children were bouncing and hopping around the room, "*Unci . . . unci*? Grandma? We're home."

A tiny gray-haired Lakota woman entered the room and sat on a chair. She smiled and put a finger to her lips to quiet the excited youngsters. They settled at her feet; the baby snuggled into her lap. The children looked expectantly at their grandmother, who began:

"Iktomi was going along. He was hungry, but he carried no bow. . . ."

FIFTEEN

The Farm

Troll could not stay with his new friend the nisse, for the humans who ranched in the foothills were strangers. But he visited every day, returning to the cave at night. Troll was so delighted and pleased to have a kindred being to talk with that he did not notice Iktomi's long absence from the cave. When he finally missed the trickster, Troll was not alarmed. "He is probably off on one of his jaunts," Troll reasoned.

But spring turned to summer and Iktomi did not return. Troll began to worry about his companion of so many years. "Perhaps some foolish human has shot Iktomi. I'd better look for him."

Troll's visits to the nisse had given him courage to venture from the cave. He saw for himself what Iktomi had reported over the years: thousands of humans in the Black Hills with houses, churches, shops, mines, and strange vehicles speeding through narrow mountain roads. Troll did not like what he saw and retreated to the less-populated foothills.

"Have you seen Iktomi?" Troll asked the nisse, who shook his head. "I fear some harm has come to him."

"Perhaps he has gone to the Indians," the nisse said, pointing east over the plains. "There are many living on the reservation."

"Yah." Troll agreed that was what Iktomi would do. "He is always looking for the Lakota."

The giant timidly ventured onto the prairie, but his fear of the vast spaces vanished at the changes he saw in the land.

Prairies he remembered as being barren and lifeless were now dotted with herds of grazing cattle. Here and there were ranches with neat houses, barns, and small gardens. Soon his long strides brought him to the muddy river that he had crossed in that terrible blizzard when he believed he had gone mad. Could these be the same waters? Troll wondered as he strolled the shores of deep blue lakes that made him think of Norway's fjords.

Gazing across the river, Troll saw that the eastern plains were also transformed. "Trees!" he exclaimed, delighting in the sight of orderly rows of trees bordering farmsteads beside field after field of fenced crops.

"I wonder what happened at Thor's farm?" Troll mused. Suddenly he was aware that the dreadful muteness, when he couldn't hear himself speak, had returned. "Not again!" he moaned.

He turned and headed back toward the Black Hills, but stopped and slowly faced east again. "It will always be there," he said, thinking of the cave. "I can find my way back if I have to. Now I need to know about Thor, Oline, and Olaf." He lengthened his stride.

The sun's heat was on his back when Troll recognized the knoll from which he had kept watch over his humans. "Some things will never change in this land," he grumbled as he wiped his sweaty brow and rubbed his sunburned nose. He gazed at the farm below. He would not have recognized it if he hadn't found the knoll.

A tidy white fence separated the house's yard from a big red barn and several smaller buildings. Within the fence was a white house, part of which Troll recognized as the one he had helped Thor build. Now a larger two-story addition was connected to the smaller building. He studied the farm and saw a boy and girl running to the yard. They opened the fence gate and called to a woman who had come out onto the wide porch of the house. Troll's heart sank as he listened to the children's chatter, for they were not speaking Norwegian. He concentrated, willing himself to understand. "Come," he heard the mother say, "wash up for supper."

As the mother and children moved to the house, a noisy moving vehicle came into the farmyard from a nearby field. The boy and girl waved to the man riding the machine. The vehicle growled to a stop, the man jumped to the ground and took off his cap. Troll rubbed his eyes. "Svend?"

No, Troll shook his head. This man was much younger, but the resemblance to the farmer in Norway was striking.

Troll rested on the smooth, green grass near the porch. He happily watched the children at play until the mother and father walked to the barn. Troll followed and found the couple milking cows. His mouth watered at the aroma of warm, fresh milk. His heart was content as he watched the couple at their evening chores. He felt as if he had come home, even if it was not Norway. He could not tear his eyes away from the man who looked so much like Svend.

The chores were done. "Time for bed," the mother called.

"Oh, not yet," the boy begged.

"Please, let us stay up a while longer?" pled the girl.

"Grandpa Olaf promised to tell us a story."

"Olaf?" Troll wondered aloud, and he jumped because he could hear himself speak. He stared at the old man seated on the porch. "Can it be?" Troll asked, and the mother lifted her head and peered into the deepening dusk.

The children ran to their grandfather. "What did you say?" they asked, puzzled at the unfamiliar sound faintly rumbling in the yard.

The old man smiled at the children and began his story. "Once, long ago in Norway, a mother asked a troll to travel to America with her children. . . ."

SIXTEEN

The Legend of the Cave

It is said that there is a cave in the Needle Spires of the Black Hills where mysterious beings live. Brave men and women have dared the dangers of the region and found the cave with signs of recent habitation. Khaki blankets were placed as if for a bed, cold ashes lay in a fire pit, and a small Lakota hand drum sat on a stone ledge. Outside the cave was a large rock with a smooth, polished depression. The puzzled visitors thought it looked like a seat for a giant.

The humans left to tell others of their discovery and returned with more explorers, but now they could not reach the cave. Thunder roared, though there were no clouds in the sky. Boulders crashed and rocks fell dangerously near. Pine cones pelted their heads and shoulders.

The people fled. They told of their fright to oldtimers in the Black Hills. These oldsters chuckled and nodded. "Yup," they recalled, "that place up in the Needles is a spooky spot. Thunder, rock slides, pine cones raining down—Long as I've been around, that's been a spooky place."

The story spread across the land, and more men and women were compelled to discover the cause of the strange occurrences. Sometimes the visitors were able to reach the cave without anything unusual happening. Other times, explorers were driven away by the thunder, crashing boulders, and a hail of pine cones. Many swore to hearing laughter as they fled.

Undaunted, the curious still come, and their reports enhance the mystery. Some say they've seen a lithe Indian male leaping through the spires. Others have glimpsed a giant before he disappeared into the cave. A few claim to have heard an Indian singing to a muffled drumbeat and at the same time a deep bass trolling a Norwegian folk song.

So it is said.

GLOSSARY

Lakota (Sioux)

ble (bleh) : lake

hau (how) : a greeting

hinh (heenh) : an expletive like "oh"

kola (koh-lah) : friend

mahto (mah-toh) : bear

Minishosha or Miniśośe (Meh-nee-sho-shay) : Missouri River

Paha Sapa (pah-hah-sah-pah) : Black Hills

tatanka (tah-tahn-kah) : buffalo

típsila (teehp-see-lah) : wild turnip

unci (oohn-chee) : grandmother

wambli (wahm-blee) : eagle

waśicu (wah-shee-choo) : white man, white person

waśte (wash-teh) : good

wińyan (wee-yohn) : woman

witko (whit-koh) : fool

Iktomi (ehk-toh-mee) : Spider Man, the name of the trickster

Norwegian

bunad (boo-nah) : dress of a particular district in Norway (each district had its own style)

fatigmand or fattigmann (fah-teh-mahn) : Christmas cookie

hulder (hool-dare) : a beautiful, wicked female with a cow's tail

Indianer (in-dee-ahn-air) : American Indian

nei (nay) : no

nei da (nay dah) : oh no, no indeed

nisse (nee-seh) : pixie or puck

nøkk (nuk : *u* as in *pearl* or *bird*) : water sprite

rømmegrøt or rømmegraut (rohm-meh-grout) : cream porridge delicacy

stabbur (stuh-boor) : storehouse on rocks or stilts in a farmyard

velkommen (vel-koh-mehn) : welcome

Source notes

The Lakota was taken from the *Dakota-English Dictionary* (Ft. Pierre SD: Working Indians Civil Association, 1969). The Norwegian usage was recommended by Dr. Carl Sunde, Scandinavian Studies, Foreign Language Department, South Dakota State University, Brookings SD. The folk songs "Å kjøre vatten" and "Hør det kaller" are as found in the *Sons of Norway Song Book* (Minneapolis MN : Sons of Norway, 1968).